Penguin Modern Classics
Bernice Bobs Her Hair and Other Stories

In Scott Fitzgerald, as in every writer of genius, there was something of the seer. He gave a name to an age – the Jazz Age – lived through that age, and saw it burn itself out. As a *New York Times* editorial stated after his death: 'He was better than he knew, for in fact and in the literary sense he invented a "generation" . . . he might have interpreted them and even guided them, as in their middle years they saw a different and nobler freedom threatened with destruction.'

F. Scott Fitzgerald was born in St Paul, Minnesota, and even as a schoolboy in St Paul he was writing, and later at Princeton. In 1917 he left Princeton for the army – but didn't get to France – and wrote in his spare moments. Then came *This Side of Paradise* – the first of his novels – followed by two volumes of short stories, and at last *The Great Gatsby*, which alone would assure Scott Fitzgerald's place among our writers of major stature. He died in 1941.

Besides *The Great Gatsby* and *This Side of Paradise* he wrote three other novels, *The Beautiful and Damned*, *Tender is the Night*, and *The Last Tycoon* (his last and unfinished work); four volumes of short stories; and *The Crack-Up*, a selection of his autobiographical pieces.

The Stories of F. Scott Fitzgerald

Volume 4

Bernice Bobs Her Hair

and Other Stories

Penguin Books

Penguin Books Ltd, Harmondsworth, Middlesex, England
Viking Penguin Inc., 40 West 23rd Street, New York, New York 10010, U.S.A.
Penguin Books Australia Ltd, Ringwood, Victoria, Australia
Penguin Books Canada Limited, 2801 John Street, Markham, Ontario, Canada L3R 1B4
Penguin Books (N.Z.) Ltd, 182–190 Wairau Road, Auckland 10, New Zealand

'Bernice Bobs Her Hair' first published 1920
'Winter Dreams' first published 1922
' "The Sensible Thing" ' first published 1924
'Absolution' first published 1924
'The Baby Party' first published 1925
'A Short Trip Home' first published 1927
'Magnetism' first published 1928
'The Rough Crossing' first published 1929
Published by The Bodley Head in
The Bodley Head Scott Fitzgerald Volume 5, 1963
Published in Penguin Books 1968
Reprinted 1974, 1976, 1978, 1982, 1984, 1986

Made and printed in Great Britain by
Hazell Watson & Viney Limited,
Member of the BPCC Group,
Aylesbury, Bucks
Set in Linotype Pilgrim

Contents

Bernice Bobs Her Hair

I

After dark on Saturday night one could stand on the first tee of the golf-course and see the country-club windows as a yellow expanse over a very black and wavy ocean. The waves of this ocean, so to speak, were the heads of many curious caddies, a few of the more ingenious chauffeurs, the golf professional's deaf sister – and there were usually several stray, diffident waves who might have rolled inside had they so desired. This was the gallery.

The balcony was inside. It consisted of the circle of wicker chairs that lined the wall of the combination club-room and ballroom. At these Saturday-night dances it was largely feminine; a great babel of middle-aged ladies with sharp eyes and icy hearts behind lorgnettes and large bosoms. The main function of the balcony was critical. It occasionally showed grudging admiration, but never approval, for it is well known among ladies over thirty-five that when the younger set dance in the summer-time it is with the very worst intentions in the world, and if they are not bombarded with stony eyes stray couples will dance weird barbaric interludes in the corners, and the more popular, more dangerous, girls will sometimes be kissed in the parked limousines of unsuspecting dowagers.

But, after all, this critical circle is not close enough to the stage to see the actors' faces and catch the subtler byplay. It can only frown and lean, ask questions and make satisfactory deductions from its set of postulates, such as the one which states that every young man with a large income leads the life of a hunted partridge. It never really appreciates the drama of the shifting, semi-cruel world of adolescence. No; boxes, orchestra-circle, principals, and chorus are represented by the medley of faces and voices that sway to the plaintive African rhythm of Dyer's dance orchestra.

From sixteen-year-old Otis Ormonde, who has two more years at Hill School, to G. Reece Stoddard, over whose bureau at home hangs a Harvard law diploma; from little Madeleine Hogue, whose hair still feels strange and uncomfortable on top of her head, to Bessie MacRae, who has been the life of the party a little too long – more than ten years – the medley is not only the centre of the stage but contains the only people capable of getting an unobstructed view of it.

With a flourish and a bang the music stops. The couples exchange artificial, effortless smiles, facetiously repeat 'la-de-da-da dum-dum,' and then the clatter of young feminine voices soars over the burst of clapping.

A few disappointed stags caught in midfloor as they had been about to cut in subsided listlessly back to the walls, because this was not like the riotous Christmas dances – these summer hops were considered just pleasantly warm and exciting, where even the younger marrieds rose and performed ancient waltzes and terrifying fox trots to the tolerant amusement of their younger brothers and sisters.

Warren McIntyre, who casually attended Yale, being one of the unfortunate stags, felt in his dinner-coat pocket for a cigarette and strolled out onto the wide, semi-dark veranda, where couples were scattered at tables, filling the lantern-hung night with vague words and hazy laughter. He nodded here and there at the less absorbed and as he passed each couple some half-forgotten fragment of a story played in his mind, for it was not a large city and everyone was Who's Who to every one else's past. There, for example, were Jim Strain and Ethel Demorest, who had been privately engaged for three years. Everyone knew that as soon as Jim managed to hold a job for more than two months she would marry him. Yet how bored they both looked, and how wearily Ethel regarded Jim sometimes, as if she wondered why she had trained the vines of her affection on such a wind-shaken poplar.

Warren was nineteen and rather pitying with those of his

friends who hadn't gone East to college. But, like most boys, he bragged tremendously about the girls of his city when he was away from it. There was Genevieve Ormonde, who regularly made the rounds of dances, house-parties, and football games at Princeton, Yale, Williams, and Cornell; there was black-eyed Roberta Dillon, who was quite as famous to her own generation as Hiram Johnson or Ty Cobb; and, of course, there was Marjorie Harvey, who besides having a fairylike face and a dazzling, bewildering tongue was already justly celebrated for having turned five cart-wheels in succession during the past pump-and-slipper dance at New Haven.

Warren, who had grown up across the street from Marjorie, had long been 'crazy about her'. Sometimes she seemed to reciprocate his feeling with a faint gratitude, but she had tried him by her infallible test and informed him gravely that she did not love him. Her test was that when she was away from him she forgot him and had affairs with other boys. Warren found this discouraging, especially as Marjorie had been making little trips all summer, and for the first two or three days after each arrival home he saw great heaps of mail on the Harveys' hall table addressed to her in various masculine handwritings. To make matters worse, all during the month of August she had been visited by her cousin Bernice from Eau Claire, and it seemed impossible to see her alone. It was always necessary to hunt round and find some one to take care of Bernice. As August waned this was becoming more and more difficult.

Much as Warren worshipped Marjorie, he had to admit that Cousin Bernice was sorta dopeless. She was pretty, with dark hair and high colour, but she was no fun on a party. Every Saturday night he danced a long arduous duty dance with her to please Marjorie, but he had never been anything but bored in her company.

'Warren' – a soft voice at his elbow broke in upon his thoughts, and he turned to see Marjorie, flushed and radiant as usual. She laid a hand on his shoulder and a glow settled almost imperceptibly over him.

'Warren,' she whispered, 'do something for me – dance with Bernice. She's been stuck with little Otis Ormonde for almost an hour.'

Warren's glow faded.

'Why – sure,' he answered half-heartedly.

'You don't mind, do you? I'll see that you don't get stuck.'

' 'Sall right.'

Marjorie smiled – that smile that was thanks enough.

'You're an angel, and I'm obliged loads.'

With a sigh the angel glanced round the veranda, but Bernice and Otis were not in sight. He wandered back inside, and there in front of the women's dressing-room he found Otis in the centre of a group of young men who were convulsed with laughter. Otis was brandishing a piece of timber he had picked up, and discoursing volubly.

'She's gone in to fix her hair,' he announced wildly. 'I'm waiting to dance another hour with her.'

Their laughter was renewed.

'Why don't some of you cut in?' cried Otis resentfully. 'She likes more variety.'

'Why, Otis,' suggested a friend, 'you've just barely got used to her.'

'Why the two-by-four, Otis?' inquired Warren, smiling.

'The two-by-four? Oh, this? This is a club. When she comes out I'll hit her on the head and knock her in again.'

Warren collapsed on a settee and howled with glee.

'Never mind, Otis,' he articulated finally. 'I'm relieving you this time.'

Otis simulated a sudden fainting attack and handed the stick to Warren.

'If you need it, old man,' he said hoarsely.

No matter how beautiful or brilliant a girl may be, the reputation of not being frequently cut in on makes her position at a dance unfortunate. Perhaps boys prefer her company to that of the butterflies with whom they dance a dozen times an evening, but youth in this jazz-nourished generation is temperamentally restless, and the idea of fox-trotting more than one full fox trot with the same girl is distasteful, not to say odious. When it comes to several dances and the intermissions between she can be quite sure that a young man, once relieved, will never tread on her wayward toes again.

Warren danced the next full dance with Bernice, and finally, thankful for the intermission, he led her to a table on the veranda. There was a moment's silence while she did unimpressive things with her fan.

'It's hotter here than in Eau Claire,' she said.

Warren stifled a sigh and nodded. It might be for all he knew or cared. He wondered idly whether she was a poor conversationalist because she got no attention or got no attention because she was a poor conversationalist.

'You going to be here much longer?' he asked, and then turned rather red. She might suspect his reasons for asking.

'Another week,' she answered, and stared at him as if to lunge at his next remark when it left his lips.

Warren fidgeted. Then with a sudden charitable impulse he decided to try part of his line on her. He turned and looked at her eyes.

'You've got an awfully kissable mouth,' he began quietly.

This was a remark that he sometimes made to girls at college proms when they were talking in just such half dark as this. Bernice distinctly jumped. She turned an ungraceful red and became clumsy with her fan. No one had ever made such a remark to her before.

'Fresh!' – the word had slipped out before she realized it, and she bit her lip. Too late she decided to be amused, and offered him a flustered smile.

Warren was annoyed. Though not accustomed to have that remark taken seriously, still it usually provoked a laugh or a paragraph of sentimental banter. And he hated to be called fresh, except in a joking way. His charitable impulse died and he switched the topic.

'Jim Strain and Ethel Demorest sitting out as usual,' he commented.

This was more in Bernice's line, but a faint regret mingled

with her relief as the subject changed. Men did not talk to her about kissable mouths, but she knew that they talked in some such way to other girls.

'Oh, yes,' she said, and laughed. 'I hear they've been moon-ing round for years without a red penny. Isn't it silly?'

Warren's disgust increased. Jim Strain was a close friend of his brother's, and anyway he considered it bad form to sneer at people for not having money. But Bernice had had no inten-tion of sneering. She was merely nervous.

2

When Marjorie and Bernice reached home at half after midnight they said good night at the top of the stairs. Though cousins, they were not intimates. As a matter of fact Marjorie had no female intimates – she considered girls stupid. Bernice on the contrary all through this parent-arranged visit had rather longed to exchange those confidences flavoured with giggles and tears that she considered an indispensable factor in all feminine intercourse. But in this respect she found Marjorie rather cold; felt somehow the same difficulty in talking to her that she had in talking to men. Marjorie never giggled, was never frightened, seldom embarrassed, and in fact had very few of the qualities which Bernice considered appropriately and blessedly feminine.

As Bernice busied herself with tooth-brush and paste this night she wondered for the hundredth time why she never had any attention when she was away from home. That her family were the wealthiest in Eau Claire; that her mother entertained tremendously, gave little dinners for her daughter before all dances and bought her a car of her own to drive round in, never occurred to her as factors in her home-town social success. Like most girls she had been brought up on the warm milk prepared by Annie Fellows Johnston and on novels in which the female was beloved because of certain mysterious womanly qualities, always mentioned but never displayed.

Bernice felt a vague pain that she was not at present engaged in being popular. She did not know that had it not been for Marjorie's campaigning she would have danced the entire evening with one man; but she knew that even in Eau Claire other girls with less position and less pulchritude were given a much bigger rush. She attributed this to something subtly unscrupulous in those girls. It had never worried her, and if it had her mother would have assured her that the other girls cheapened themselves and that men really respected girls like Bernice.

She turned out the light in her bathroom, and on an impulse decided to go in and chat for a moment with her aunt Josephine whose light was still on. Her soft slippers bore her noiselessly down the carpeted hall, but hearing voices inside she stopped near the partly opened door. Then she caught her own name, and without any definite intention of eavesdropping lingered – and the thread of the conversation going on inside pierced her consciousness sharply as if it had been drawn through with a needle.

'She's absolutely hopeless!' It was Marjorie's voice. 'Oh, I know what you're going to say! So many people have told you how pretty and sweet she is, and how she can cook! What of it? She has a bum time. Men don't like her.'

'What's a little cheap popularity?'

Mrs Harvey sounded annoyed.

'It's everything when you're eighteen,' said Marjorie emphatically. 'I've done my best. I've been polite and I've made men dance with her, but they just won't stand being bored. When I think of that gorgeous colouring wasted on such a ninny, and think what Martha Carey could do with it – oh!'

'There's no courtesy these days.'

Mrs Harvey's voice implied that modern situations were too much for her. When she was a girl all young ladies who belonged to nice families had glorious times.

'Well,' said Marjorie, 'no girl can permanently bolster up a lame-duck visitor, because these days it's every girl for herself. I've even tried to drop her hints about clothes and things, and she's been furious – given me the funniest looks. She's sensitive enough to know she's not getting away with much, but I'll bet she consoles herself by thinking that she's very virtuous and that I'm too gay and fickle and will come to a bad end. All unpopular girls think that way. Sour grapes! Sarah Hopkins refers to Genevieve and Roberta and me as gardenia girls! I'll bet she'd give ten years of her life and her European education to be a gardenia girl and have three or four men in love with her and be cut in on every few feet at dances.'

'It seems to me,' interrupted Mrs Harvey rather wearily, 'that you ought to be able to do something for Bernice. I know she's not very vivacious.'

Marjorie groaned.

'Vivacious! Good grief! I've never heard her say anything to a boy except that it's hot or the floor's crowded or that she's going to school in New York next year. Sometimes she asks them what kind of car they have and tells them the kind she has. Thrilling!'

There was a short silence, and then Mrs Harvey took up her refrain:

'All I know is that other girls not half so sweet and attractive get partners. Martha Carey, for instance, is stout and loud, and her mother is distinctly common. Roberta Dillon is so thin this year that she looks as though Arizona were the place for her. She's dancing herself to death.'

'But, mother,' objected Marjorie impatiently, 'Martha is cheerful and awfully witty and an awfully slick girl, and Roberta's a marvellous dancer. She's been popular for ages!'

Mrs Harvey yawned.

'I think it's that crazy Indian blood in Bernice,' continued Marjorie. 'Maybe she's a reversion to type. Indian women all just sat round and never said anything.'

'Go to bed, you silly child,' laughed Mrs Harvey. 'I wouldn't have told you that if I'd thought you were going to remember it. And I think most of your ideas are perfectly idiotic,' she finished sleepily.

There was another silence, while Marjorie considered whether or not convincing her mother was worth the trouble.

People over forty can seldom be permanently convinced of anything. At eighteen our convictions are hills from which we look; at forty-five they are caves in which we hide.

Having decided this, Marjorie said good night. When she came out into the hall it was quite empty .

3

While Marjorie was breakfasting late next day Bernice came into the room with a rather formal good morning, sat down opposite, stared intently over and slightly moistened her lips.

'What's on your mind?' inquired Marjorie, rather puzzled.

Bernice paused before she threw her hand-grenade.

'I heard what you said about me to your mother last night.'

Marjorie was startled, but she showed only a faintly heightened colour and her voice was quite even when she spoke.

'Where were you?'

'In the hall. I didn't mean to listen – at first.'

After an involuntary look of contempt Marjorie dropped her eyes and became very interested in balancing a stray corn-flake on her finger.

'I guess I'd better go back to Eau Claire – if I'm such a nuisance.' Bernice's lower lip was trembling violently and she continued on a wavering note: 'I've tried to be nice, and – and I've been first neglected and then insulted. No one ever visited me and got such treatment.'

Marjorie was silent.

'But I'm in the way, I see. I'm a drag on you. Your friends don't like me.' She paused, and then remembered another one of her grievances. 'Of course I was furious last week when you tried to hint to me that that dress was unbecoming. Don't you think I know how to dress myself?'

'No,' murmured Marjorie less than half-aloud.

'What?'

'I didn't hint anything,' said Marjorie succinctly. 'I said, as I remember, that it was better to wear a becoming dress three times straight than to alternate it with two frights.'

'Do you think that was a very nice thing to say?'

'I wasn't trying to be nice.' Then after a pause: 'When do you want to go?'

Bernice drew in her breath sharply.

'Oh!' It was a little half-cry.

Marjorie looked up in surprise.

'Didn't you say you were going?'

'Yes, but —'

'Oh, you were only bluffing!'

They stared at each other across the breakfast-table for a moment. Misty waves were passing before Bernice's eyes, while Marjorie's face wore that rather hard expression that she used when slightly intoxicated undergraduates were making love to her.

'So you were bluffing,' she repeated as if it were what she might have expected.

Bernice admitted it by bursting into tears. Marjorie's eyes showed boredom.

'You're my cousin,' sobbed Bernice. 'I'm v-v-visiting you. I was to stay a month, and if I go home my mother will know and she'll wah-wonder —'

Marjorie waited until the shower of broken words collapsed into little sniffles.

'I'll give you my month's allowance,' she said coldly, and 'you can spend this last week anywhere you want. There's a very nice hotel —'

Bernice's sobs rose to a flute note, and rising of a sudden she fled from the room.

An hour later, while Marjorie was in the library absorbed in composing one of those non-committal, marvellously elusive letters that only a young girl can write, Bernice reappeared, very red-eyed and consciously calm. She cast no glance at Marjorie but took a book at random from the shelf and sat down as if to read. Marjorie seemed absorbed in her letter and continued writing. When the clock showed noon Bernice closed her book with a snap.

'I suppose I'd better get my railroad ticket.'

This was not the beginning of the speech she had rehearsed upstairs, but as Marjorie was not getting her cues – wasn't urging her to be reasonable; it's all a mistake – it was the best opening she could muster.

'Just wait till I finish this letter,' said Marjorie without looking round. 'I want to get it off in the next mail.'

After another minute, during which her pen scratched busily, she turned round and relaxed with an air of 'at your service'. Again Bernice had to speak.

'Do you want me to go home?'

'Well,' said Marjorie, considering, 'I suppose if you're not having a good time you'd better go. No use being miserable.'

'Don't you think common kindness –'

'Oh, please don't quote "Little Women"!' cried Marjorie impatiently. 'That's out of style.'

'You think so?'

'Heavens, yes! What modern girl could live like those inane females?'

'They were the models for our mothers.'

Marjorie laughed.

'Yes, they were – not! Besides, our mothers were all very well in their way, but they know very little about their daughters' problems.'

Bernice drew herself up.

'Please don't talk about my mother.'

Marjorie laughed.

'I don't think I mentioned her.'

Bernice felt that she was being led away from her subject.

'Do you think you've treated me very well?'

'I've done my best. You're rather hard material to work with.'

The lids of Bernice's eyes reddened.

'I think you're hard and selfish, and you haven't a feminine quality in you.'

'Oh, my Lord!' cried Marjorie in desperation. 'You little nut! Girls like you are responsible for all the tiresome colourless marriages; all those ghastly inefficiencies that pass as feminine qualities. What a blow it must be when a man with imagination marries the beautiful bundle of clothes that he's been building ideals round, and finds that she's just a weak, whining, cowardly mass of affectations!'

Bernice's mouth had slipped half open.

'The womanly woman!' continued Marjorie. 'Her whole early life is occupied in whining criticisms of girls like me who really do have a good time.'

Bernice's jaw descended farther as Marjorie's voice rose.

'There's some excuse for an ugly girl whining. If I'd been irretrievably ugly I'd never have forgiven my parents for bringing me into the world. But you're starting life without any handicap –' Marjorie's little fist clinched. 'If you expect me to weep with you you'll be disappointed. Go or stay, just as you like.' And picking up her letters she left the room.

Bernice claimed a headache and failed to appear at luncheon. They had a matinée date for the afternoon, but the headache persisting, Marjorie made explanations to a not very downcast boy. But when she returned late in the afternoon she found Bernice with a strangely set face waiting for her in her bed-room.

'I've decided,' began Bernice without preliminaries, 'that maybe you're right about things – possibly not. But if you'll tell me why your friends aren't – aren't interested in me, I'll see if I can do what you want me to.'

Marjorie was at the mirror shaking down her hair.

'Do you mean it?'

'Yes.'

'Without reservations? Will you do exactly what I say?'

'Well, I –'

'Well nothing! Will you do exactly as I say?'

'If they're sensible things.'

'They're not! You're no case for sensible things.'

'Are you going to make – to recommend –'

'Yes, everything. If I tell you to take boxing lessons you'll have to do it. Write home and tell your mother you're going to stay another two weeks.'

'If you'll tell me –'

'All right – I'll just give you a few examples now. First, you have no ease of manner. Why? Because you're never sure about your personal appearance. When a girl feels that she's perfectly groomed and dressed she can forget that part of her. That's charm. The more parts of yourself you can afford to forget the more charm you have.'

'Don't I look all right?'

'No; for instance, you never take care of your eyebrows. They're black and lustrous, but by leaving them straggly they're a blemish. They'd be beautiful if you'd take care of them in one-tenth of the time you take doing nothing. You're going to brush them so that they'll grow straight.'

Bernice raised the brows in question.

'Do you mean to say that men notice eyebrows?'

'Yes – subconsciously. And when you go home you ought to have your teeth straightened a little. It's almost imperceptible, still –'

'But I thought,' interrupted Bernice in bewilderment, 'that you despised little dainty feminine things like that.'

'I hate dainty minds,' answered Marjorie. 'But a girl has to be dainty in person. If she looks like a million dollars she can talk about Russia, ping-pong, or the League of Nations and get away with it.'

'What else?'

'Oh, I'm just beginning! There's your dancing.'

'Don't I dance all right?'

'No, you don't – you lean on a man; yes, you do – ever so slightly. I noticed it when we were dancing together yesterday. And you dance standing up straight instead of bending over a little. Probably some old lady on the sideline once told you that you looked so dignified that way. But except with a very small girl it's much harder on the man, and he's the one that counts.'

'Go on.' Bernice's brain was reeling.

'Well, you've got to learn to be nice to men who are sad birds. You look as if you'd been insulted whenever you're thrown with any except the most popular boys. Why, Bernice, I'm cut in on every few feet – and who does most of it? Why, those very sad birds. No girl can afford to neglect them. They're the big part of any crowd. Young boys too shy to talk are the very best conversational practice. Clumsy boys are the best dancing practice. If you can follow them and yet look graceful you can follow a baby tank across a barb-wire sky-scraper.'

Bernice sighed profoundly, but Marjorie was not through.

'If you go to a dance and really amuse, say, three sad birds that dance with you; if you talk so well to them that they forget they're stuck with you, you've done something. They'll come back next time, and gradually so many sad birds will dance with you that the attractive boys will see there's no danger of being stuck – then they'll dance with you.'

'Yes,' agreed Bernice faintly. 'I think I begin to see.'

'And finally,' concluded Marjorie, 'poise and charm will just come. You'll wake up some morning knowing you've attained it, and men will know it too.'

Bernice rose.

'It's been awfully kind of you – but nobody's ever talked to me like this before, and I feel sort of startled.'

Marjorie made no answer but gazed pensively at her own image in the mirror.

'You're a peach to help me,' continued Bernice.

Still Marjorie did not answer, and Bernice thought she had seemed too grateful.

'I know you don't like sentiment,' she said timidly.

Marjorie turned to her quickly.

'Oh, I wasn't thinking about that. I was considering whether we hadn't better bob your hair.'

Bernice collapsed backward upon the bed.

4

On the following Wednesday evening there was a dinner-dance at the country club. When the guests strolled in Bernice found her place-card with a slight feeling of irritation. Though at her right sat G. Reece Stoddard, a most desirable and distinguished young bachelor, the all-important left held only Charley Paulson. Charley lacked height, beauty, and social shrewdness, and in her new enlightenment Bernice decided that his only qualification to be her partner was that he had never been stuck with her. But this feeling of irritation left with the last of the soup-plates, and Marjorie's specific instruction came to her. Swallowing her pride she turned to Charley Paulson and plunged.

'Do you think I ought to bob my hair, Mr Charley Paulson?'

Charley looked up in surprise.

'Why?'

'Because I'm considering it. It's such a sure and easy way of attracting attention.'

Charley smiled pleasantly. He could not know this had been rehearsed. He replied that he didn't know much about bobbed hair. But Bernice was there to tell him.

'I want to be a society vampire, you see,' she announced coolly, and went on to inform him that bobbed hair was the necessary prelude. She added that she wanted to ask his advice, because she had heard he was so critical about girls.

Charley, who knew as much about the psychology of women as he did of the mental states of Buddhist contemplatives, felt vaguely flattered.

'So I've decided,' she continued, her voice rising slightly, 'that early next week I'm going down to the Sevier Hotel barber-shop, sit in the first chair, and get my hair bobbed.' She faltered, noticing that the people near her had paused in their conversation and were listening; but after a confused second Marjorie's coaching told, and she finished her paragraph to the vicinity at large. 'Of course I'm charging admission, but if you'll all come down and encourage me I'll issue passes for the inside seats.'

There was a ripple of appreciative laughter, and under cover of it G. Reece Stoddard leaned over quickly and said to her ear: 'I'll take a box right now.'

She met his eyes and smiled as if he had said something surpassingly brilliant.

'Do you believe in bobbed hair?' asked G. Reece in the same undertone .

'I think it's unmoral,' affirmed Bernice gravely. 'But, of course, you've either got to amuse people or feed 'em or shock 'em.' Marjorie had culled this from Oscar Wilde. It was greeted with a ripple of laughter from the men and a series of quick, intent looks from the girls. And then as though she had said nothing of wit or moment Bernice turned again to Charley and spoke confidentially in his ear.

'I want to ask you your opinion of several people. I imagine you're a wonderful judge of character.'

Charley thrilled faintly – paid her a subtle compliment by overturning her water.

Two hours later, while Warren McIntyre was standing passively in the stag line abstractedly watching the dancers and wondering whither and with whom Marjorie had disappeared, an unrelated perception began to creep slowly upon him – a perception that Bernice, cousin to Marjorie, had been cut in on several times in the past five minutes. He closed his eyes, opened them and looked again. Several minutes back she had been dancing with a visiting boy, a matter easily accounted for; a visiting boy would know no better. But now she was dancing with some one else, and there was Charley Paulson headed for her with enthusiastic determination in his eye. Funny – Charley seldom danced with more than three girls an evening.

Warren was distinctly surprised when – the exchange having been effected – the man relieved proved to be none other than G. Reece Stoddard himself. And G. Reece seemed not at all jubilant at being relieved. Next time Bernice danced near, Warren regarded her intently. Yes, she was pretty, distinctly pretty; and tonight her face seemed really vivacious. She had that look that no woman, however histrionically proficient, can successfully counterfeit – she looked as if she were having a good time. He liked the way she had her hair arranged, wondering if it was brilliantine that made it glisten so. And that dress was becoming – a dark red that set off her shadowy eyes and high colouring. He remembered that he had thought her pretty when she first came to town, before he had realized that she was dull. Too bad she was dull – dull girls were unbearable – certainly pretty though.

His thoughts zigzagged back to Marjorie. This disappearance would be like other disappearances. When she reappeared he would demand where she had been – would be told emphatically that it was none of his business. What a pity she was so sure of him! She basked in the knowledge that no other girl in town interested him; she defied him to fall in love with Genevieve or Roberta.

Warren sighed. The way to Marjorie's affections was a labyrinth indeed. He looked up. Bernice was again dancing with the visiting boy. Half unconsciously he took a step out from the stag line in her direction, and hesitated. Then he said to himself that it was charity. He walked towards her – collided suddenly with G. Reece Stoddard.

'Pardon me,' said Warren.

But G. Reece had not stopped to apologize. He had again cut in on Bernice.

That night at one o'clock Marjorie, with one hand on the electric-light switch in the hall, turned to take a last look at Bernice's sparkling eyes.

'So it worked?'

'Oh, Marjorie, yes!' cried Bernice.

'I saw you were having a gay time.'

'I did! The only trouble was that about midnight I ran short of talk. I had to repeat myself – with different men of course. I hope they won't compare notes.'

'Men don't,' said Marjorie, yawning, 'and it wouldn't matter if they did – they'd think you were even trickier.'

She snapped out the light, and as they started up the stairs Bernice grasped the banister thankfully. For the first time in her life she had been danced tired.

'You see,' said Marjorie at the top of the stairs, 'one man

sees another man cut in and he thinks there must be something there. Well, we'll fix up some new stuff tomorrow. Good night.'

'Good night.'

As Bernice took down her hair she passed the evening before her in review. She had followed instructions exactly. Even when Charley Paulson cut in for the eighth time she had simulated delight and had apparently been both interested and flattered. She had not talked about the weather or Eau Claire or automobiles or her school, but had confined her conversation to me, you, and us.

But a few minutes before she fell asleep a rebellious thought was churning drowsily in her brain – after all, it was she who had done it. Marjorie, to be sure, had given her her conversation, but then Marjorie got much of her conversation out of things she read. Bernice had bought the red dress, though she had never valued it highly before Marjorie dug it out of her trunk – and her own voice had said the words, her own lips had smiled, her own feet had danced. Marjorie nice girl – vain, though – nice evening – nice boys – like Warren – Warren – Warren – what's-his-name – Warren –

She fell asleep.

5

To Bernice the next week was a revelation. With the feeling that people really enjoyed looking at her and listening to her came the foundation of self-confidence. Of course there were numerous mistakes at first. She did not know, for instance, that Draycott Deyo was studying for the ministry; she was unaware that he had cut in on her because he thought she was a quiet, reserved girl. Had she known these things she would not have treated him to the line which began 'Hello, Shell Shock!' and continued with the bathtub story – 'It takes a frightful lot of energy to fix my hair in the summer – there's so much of it – so I always fix it first and powder my face and put on my hat; then I get into the bathtub, and dress afterwards. Don't you think that's the best plan?'

Though Draycott Deyo was in the throes of difficulties concerning baptism by immersion and might possibly have seen a connexion, it must be admitted that he did not. He considered feminine bathing an immoral subject, and gave her some of his ideas on the depravity of modern society.

But to offset that unfortunate occurrence Bernice had several signal successes to her credit. Little Otis Ormonde pleaded off from a trip East and elected instead to follow her with a puppy-like devotion, to the amusement of his crowd and to the irritation of G. Reece Stoddard, several of whose afternoon calls Otis completely ruined by the disgusting tenderness of the glances he bent on Bernice. He even told her the story of the two-by-four and the dressing-room to show her how frightfully mistaken he and everyone else had been in their first judgement of her. Bernice laughed off that incident with a slight sinking sensation.

Of all Bernice's conversation perhaps the best known and most universally approved was the line about the bobbing of her hair.

'Oh, Bernice, when you goin' to get the hair bobbed?'

'Day after tomorrow maybe,' she would reply, laughing. 'Will you come and see me? Because I'm counting on you, you know.'

'Will we? You know! But you better hurry up.'

Bernice, whose tonsorial intentions were strictly dishonourable, would laugh again.

'Pretty soon now. You'd be surprised.'

But perhaps the most significant symbol of her success was the grey car of the hypercritical Warren McIntyre, parked daily in front of the Harvey house. At first the parlourmaid was distinctly startled when he asked for Bernice instead of Marjorie; after a week of it she told the cook that Miss Bernice had gotta hold Miss Marjorie's best fella.

And Miss Bernice had. Perhaps it began with Warren's desire to rouse jealousy in Marjorie; perhaps it was the familiar though unrecognized strain of Marjorie in Bernice's conversation; perhaps it was both of these and something of sincere attraction besides. But somehow the collective mind of the younger set knew within a week that Marjorie's most reliable beau had made an amazing face-about and was giving an indisputable rush to Marjorie's guest. The question of the moment was how Marjorie would take it. Warren called Bernice on the 'phone twice a day, sent her notes, and they were frequently seen together in his roadster, obviously engrossed in one of those tense, significant conversations as to whether or not he was sincere.

Marjorie on being twitted only laughed. She said she was mighty glad that Warren had at last found someone who appreciated him. So the younger set laughed, too, and guessed that Marjorie didn't care and let it go at that.

One afternoon when there were only three days left of her visit Bernice was waiting in the hall for Warren, with whom she was going to a bridge party. She was in rather a blissful mood, and when Marjorie – also bound for the party – appeared beside her and began casually to adjust her hat in the mirror, Bernice was utterly unprepared for anything in the nature of a clash. Marjorie did her work very coldly and succinctly in three sentences.

'You may as well get Warren out of your head,' she said coldly.

'What?' Bernice was utterly astounded.

'You may as well stop making a fool of yourself over Warren McIntyre. He doesn't care a snap of his fingers about you.'

For a tense moment they regarded each other – Marjorie scornful, aloof; Bernice astounded, half-angry, half-afraid. Then two cars drove up in front of the house and there was a riotous honking. Both of them gasped faintly, turned, and side by side hurried out.

All through the bridge party Bernice strove in vain to master a rising uneasiness. She had offended Marjorie, the sphinx of sphinxes. With the most wholesome and innocent intentions in the world she had stolen Marjorie's property. She felt suddenly and horribly guilty. After the bridge game, when they sat in an informal circle and the conversation became general, the storm gradually broke. Little Otis Ormonde inadvertently precipitated it.

'When you going back to kindergarten, Otis?' some one had asked.

'Me? Day Bernice gets her hair bobbed.'

'Then your education's over,' said Marjorie quickly. 'That's only a bluff of hers. I should think you'd have realized.'

'That a fact?' demanded Otis, giving Bernice a reproachful glance.

Bernice's ears burned as she tried to think up an effectual comeback. In the face of this direct attack her imagination was paralysed.

'There's a lot of bluffs in the world,' continued Marjorie quite pleasantly. 'I should think you'd be young enough to know that, Otis.'

'Well,' said Otis, 'maybe so. But gee! With a line like Bernice's –'

'Really?' yawned Marjorie. 'What's her latest bon mot?'

No one seemed to know. In fact, Bernice, having trifled with her muse's beau, had said nothing memorable of late.

'Was that really all a line?' asked Roberta curiously.

Bernice hesitated. She felt that wit in some form was demanded of her, but under her cousin's suddenly frigid eyes she was completely incapacitated.

'I don't know,' she stalled.

'Splush!' said Marjorie. 'Admit it!'

Bernice saw that Warren's eyes had left a ukulele he had been tinkering with and were fixed on her questioningly.

'Oh, I don't know!' she repeated steadily. Her cheeks were glowing.

'Splush!' remarked Marjorie again.

'Come through, Bernice,' urged Otis. 'Tell her where to get off.'

Bernice looked round again – she seemed unable to get away from Warren's eyes.

'I like bobbed hair,' she said hurriedly, as if he had asked her a question, 'and I intend to bob mine.'

'When?' demanded Marjorie.

'Any time.'

'No time like the present,' suggested Roberta.

Otis jumped to his feet.

'Good stuff!' he cried. 'We'll have a summer bobbing party. Sevier Hotel barber-shop, I think you said.'

In an instant all were on their feet. Bernice's heart throbbed violently.

'What?' she gasped.

Out of the group came Marjorie's voice, very clear and contemptuous.

'Don't worry – she'll back out!'

'Come on, Bernice!' cried Otis, starting towards the door.

Four eyes – Warren's and Marjorie's – stared at her, challenged her, defied her. For another second she wavered wildly.

'All right,' she said swiftly, 'I don't care if I do.'

An eternity of minutes later, riding down-town through the late afternoon beside Warren, the others following in Roberta's car close behind, Bernice had all the sensations of Marie Antoinette bound for the guillotine in a tumbrel. Vaguely she wondered why she did not cry out that it was all a mistake. It was all she could do to keep from clutching her hair with both hands to protect it from the suddenly hostile world. Yet she did neither. Even the thought of her mother was no deterrent now. This was the test supreme of her sportsmanship; her right to walk unchallenged in the starry heaven of popular girls.

Warren was moodily silent, and when they came to the hotel he drew up at the kerb and nodded to Bernice to precede him out. Roberta's car emptied a laughing crowd into the shop, which presented two bold plate-glass windows to the street.

Bernice stood on the kerb and looked at the sign, Sevier Barber-Shop. It was a guillotine indeed, and the hangman was the first barber, who, attired in a white coat and smoking a cigarette, leaned nonchalantly against the first chair. He must have heard of her; he must have been waiting all week, smoking eternal cigarettes beside that portentous, too-often-mentioned first chair. Would they blindfold her? No, but they would tie a white cloth round her neck lest any of her blood – nonsense – hair – should get on her clothes.

'All right, Bernice,' said Warren quickly.

With her chin in the air she crossed the sidewalk, pushed open the swinging screen-door, and giving not a glance to the uproarious, riotous row that occupied the waiting bench, went up to the first barber.

'I want you to bob my hair.'

The first barber's mouth slid somewhat open. His cigarette dropped to the floor.

'Huh?'

'My hair – bob it!'

Refusing further preliminaries, Bernice took her seat on high. A man in the chair next to her turned on his side and gave her a glance, half lather, half amazement. One barber started and spoiled little Willy Schuneman's monthly haircut. Mr O'Reilly in the last chair grunted and swore musically in ancient Gaelic as a razor bit into his cheek. Two bootblacks became wide-eyed and rushed for her feet. No, Bernice didn't care for a shine.

Outside a passer-by stopped and stared; a couple joined him; half a dozen small boys' noses sprang into life, flattened against the glass; and snatches of conversation borne on the summer breeze drifted in through the screen-door.

'Lookada long hair on a kid!'

'Where'd yuh get 'at stuff? 'At's a bearded lady he just finished shavin'.'

But Bernice saw nothing, heard nothing. Her only living sense told her that this man in the white coat had removed one tortoiseshell comb and then another; that his fingers were fumbling clumsily with unfamiliar hairpins; that this hair, this wonderful hair of hers, was going – she would never again feel its long voluptuous pull as it hung in a dark-brown glory down her back. For a second she was near breaking down, and then the picture before her swam mechanically into her vision – Marjorie's mouth curling in a faint ironic smile as if to say:

'Give up and get down! You tried to buck me and I called your bluff. You see you haven't got a prayer.'

And some last energy rose up in Bernice, for she clenched her hands under the white cloth, and there was a curious narrowing of her eyes that Marjorie remarked on to someone long afterward.

Twenty minutes later the barber swung her round to face the mirror, and she flinched at the full extent of the damage that had been wrought. Her hair was not curly, and now it lay in lank lifeless blocks on both sides of her suddenly pale face. It was ugly as sin – she had known it would be ugly as sin. Her face's chief charm had been a Madonna-like simplicity. Now that was gone and she was – well, frightfully mediocre – not stagy; only ridiculous, like a Greenwich Villager who had left her spectacles at home.

As she climbed down from the chair she tried to smile – failed miserably. She saw two of the girls exchange glances; noticed Marjorie's mouth curved in attentuated mockery – and that Warren's eyes were suddenly very cold.

'You see' – her words fell into an awkward pause – 'I've done it.'

'Yes, you've – done it,' admitted Warren.

'Do you like it?'

There was a half-hearted 'Sure' from two or three voices, another awkward pause, and then Marjorie turned swiftly and with serpent-like intensity to Warren.

'Would you mind running me down to the cleaners?' she asked. 'I've simply got to get a dress there before supper. Roberta's driving right home and she can take the others.'

Warren stared abstractedly at some infinite speck out the window. Then for an instant his eyes rested coldly on Bernice before they turned to Marjorie.

'Be glad to,' he said slowly.

6

Bernice did not fully realize the outrageous trap that had been set for her until she met her aunt's amazed glance just before dinner.

'Why, Bernice!'

'I've bobbed it, Aunt Josephine.'

'Why, child!'

'Do you like it?'

'Why, Ber-nice!'

'I suppose I've shocked you.'

'No, but what'll Mrs Deyo think tomorrow night? Bernice, you should have waited until after the Deyos' dance – you should have waited if you wanted to do that.'

'It was sudden, Aunt Josephine. Anyway, why does it matter to Mrs Deyo particularly?'

'Why, child,' cried Mrs Harvey, 'in her paper on "The Foibles of the Younger Generation" that she read at the last meeting of the Thursday Club she devoted fifteen minutes to bobbed hair. It's her pet abomination. And the dance is for you and Marjorie!'

'I'm sorry.'

'Oh, Bernice, what'll your mother say? She'll think I let you do it.'

'I'm sorry.'

Dinner was an agony. She had made a hasty attempt with a curling-iron, and burned her finger and much hair. She could see that her aunt was both worried and grieved, and her uncle kept saying, 'Well, I'll be darned!' over and over in a hurt and faintly hostile tone. And Marjorie sat very quietly, entrenched behind a faint smile, a faintly mocking smile.

Somehow she got through the evening. Three boys called; Marjorie disappeared with one of them, and Bernice made a listless unsuccessful attempt to entertain the two others – sighed thankfully as she climbed the stairs to her room at half past ten. What a day!

When she had undressed for the night the door opened and Marjorie came in.

'Bernice,' she said, 'I'm awfully sorry about the Deyo dance. I'll give you my word of honour I'd forgotten all about it.'

''Sall right,' said Bernice shortly. Standing before the mirror she passed her comb slowly through her short hair.

'I'll take you down-town tomorrow,' continued Marjorie, 'and the hairdresser'll fix it so you'll look slick. I didn't imagine you'd go through with it. I'm really mighty sorry.'

'Oh, 'sall right!'

'Still it's your last night, so I suppose it won't matter much.'

Then Bernice winced as Marjorie tossed her own hair over her shoulders and began to twist it slowly into two long blonde braids until in her cream-coloured négligé she looked like a delicate painting of some Saxon princess. Fascinated, Bernice watched the braids grow. Heavy and luxurious they were, moving under the supple fingers like restive snakes – and to Bernice remained this relic and the curling-iron and a tomorrow full of eyes. She could see G. Reece Stoddard, who liked her, assuming his Harvard manner and telling his dinner partner that Bernice shouldn't have been allowed to go to the movies so much; she could see Draycott Deyo exchanging glances with his mother and then being conscientiously charitable to her. But then perhaps by tomorrow Mrs Deyo would have heard the news; would send round an icy little note requesting that she fail to appear – and behind her back they would all laugh and know that Marjorie had made a fool of her; that her chance at beauty had been sacrificed to the jealous whim of a selfish girl. She sat down suddenly before the mirror, biting the inside of her cheek.

'I like it,' she said with an effort. 'I think it will be becoming.'

Marjorie smiled.

'It looks all right. For heaven's sake, don't let it worry you!'

'I won't.'

'Good night, Bernice.'

But as the door closed something snapped within Bernice. She sprang dynamically to her feet, clenching her hands, then swiftly and noiselessly crossed over to her bed and from underneath it dragged out her suitcase. Into it she tossed toilet articles and a change of clothing. Then she turned to her trunk and quickly dumped in two drawerfuls of lingerie and summer dresses. She moved quietly, but with deadly efficiency, and in three-quarters of an hour her trunk was locked and strapped and she was fully dressed in a becoming new travelling suit that Marjorie had helped her pick out.

Sitting down at her desk she wrote a short note to Mrs Harvey, in which she briefly outlined her reasons for going. She sealed it, addressed it, and laid it on her pillow. She glanced at her watch. The train left at one, and she knew that if she walked down to the Marborough Hotel two blocks away she could easily get a taxicab.

Suddenly she drew in her breath sharply and an expression flashed into her eyes that a practised character reader might have connected vaguely with the set look she had worn in the barber's chair – somehow a development of it. It was quite a new look for Bernice – and it carried consequences.

She went stealthily to the bureau, picked up an article that lay there, and turning out all the lights stood quietly until her eyes became accustomed to the darkness. Softly she pushed open the door to Marjorie's room. She heard the quiet, even breathing of an untroubled conscience asleep.

She was by the bedside now, very deliberate and calm. She acted swiftly. Bending over she found one of the braids of Marjorie's hair, followed it up with her hand to the point nearest the head, and then holding it a little slack so that the sleeper would feel no pull, she reached down with the shears and severed it. With the pigtail in her hand she held her breath. Marjorie had muttered something in her sleep. Bernice deftly amputated the other braid, paused for an instant, and then flitted swiftly and silently back to her own room.

Downstairs she opened the big front door, closed it carefully behind her, and feeling oddly happy and exuberant stepped off the porch into the moonlight, swinging her heavy grip like a shopping-bag. After a minute's brisk walk she discovered that her left hand still held the two blonde braids. She laughed unexpectedly – had to shut her mouth hard to keep from emitting an absolute peal. She was passing Warren's house now, and on the impulse she set down her baggage, and swinging the braids like pieces of rope flung them at the wooden porch, where they landed with a slight thud. She laughed again, no longer restraining herself.

'Huh!' she giggled wildly. 'Scalp the selfish thing!'

Then picking up her suitcase she set off at a half-run down the moonlit street.

Winter Dreams

I

Some of the caddies were poor as sin and lived in one-room houses with a neurasthenic cow in the front yard, but Dexter Green's father owned the second-best grocery-store in Black Bear – the best one was 'The Hub', patronized by the wealthy people from Sherry Island – and Dexter caddied only for pocket-money.

In the fall when the days became crisp and grey, and the long Minnesota winter shut down like the white lid of a box, Dexter's skis moved over the snow that hid the fairways of the golf course. At these times the country gave him a feeling of profound melancholy – it offended him that the links should lie in enforced fallowness, haunted by ragged sparrows for the long season. It was dreary, too, that on the trees where the gay colours fluttered in summer there were now only the desolate sand-boxes knee-deep in crusted ice. When he crossed the hills the wind blew cold as misery, and if the sun was out he tramped with his eyes squinted up against the hard dimensionless glare.

In April the winter ceased abruptly. The snow ran down into Black Bear Lake scarcely tarrying for the early golfers to brave the season with red and black balls. Without elation, without an interval of moist glory, the cold was gone.

Dexter knew that there was something dismal about this Northern spring, just as he knew there was something gorgeous about the fall. Fall made him clench his hands and tremble and repeat idiotic sentences to himself, and make brisk abrupt gestures of command to imaginary audiences and armies. October filled him with hope which November raised to a sort of ecstatic triumph, and in this mood the fleeting brilliant impressions of the summer at Sherry Island were ready grist to his mill. He became golf champion and defeated Mr T. A. Hedrick in a marvellous match played a hundred times over the fairways of his imagination, a match each detail of which he changed about untiringly – sometimes he won with almost laughable ease, sometimes he came up magnificently from behind. Again, stepping from a Pierce-Arrow automobile, like Mr Mortimer Jones, he strolled frigidly into the lounge of the Sherry Island Golf Club – or perhaps, surrounded by an admiring crowd, he gave an exhibition of fancy diving from the springboard of the club raft.... Among those who watched in open-mouthed wonder was Mr Mortimer Jones.

And one day it came to pass that Mr Jones – himself and not his ghost – came up to Dexter with tears in his eyes and said that Dexter was the — best caddy in the club, and wouldn't he decide not to quit if Mr Jones made it worth his while, because every other — caddy in the club lost one ball a hole for him – regularly –

'No, sir,' said Dexter decisively, 'I don't want to caddy any more.' Then, after a pause : 'I'm too old.'

'You're not more than fourteen. Why the devil did you decide just this morning that you wanted to quit ? You promised that next week you'd go over to the state tournament with me.'

'I decided I was too old.'

Dexter handed in his 'A Class' badge, collected what money was due him from the caddy-master, and walked home to Black Bear Village.

'The best — caddy I ever saw,' shouted Mr Mortimer Jones over a drink that afternoon. 'Never lost a ball! Willing! Intelligent! Quiet! Honest! Grateful!'

The little girl who had done this was eleven – beautifully ugly as little girls are apt to be who are destined after a few years to be inexpressibly lovely and bring no end of misery to a great number of men. The spark however was perceptible. There was a general ungodliness in the way her lips twisted down at the corners when she smiled, and in the – Heaven help us! – in the almost passionate quality of her eyes. Vitality is born early in such women. It was utterly in evidence now, shining through her thin frame in a sort of glow.

She had come eagerly out on to the course at nine o'clock with a white linen nurse and five small new golf-clubs in a white canvas bag which the nurse was carrying. When Dexter first saw her she was standing by the caddy house, rather ill at ease and trying to conceal the fact by engaging her nurse in an obviously unnatural conversation graced by startling and irrelevant grimaces from herself.

'Well, it's certainly a nice day, Hilda,' Dexter heard her say. She drew down the corners of her mouth, smiled, and glanced furtively around, her eyes in transit falling for an instant on Dexter.

Then to the nurse :

'Well, I guess there aren't many people out here this morning, are there ?'

The smile again – radiant, blatantly artificial – convincing.

'I don't know what we're supposed to do now,' said the nurse looking nowhere in particular.

'Oh, that's all right. I'll fix it up.'

Dexter stood perfectly still, his mouth slightly ajar. He knew that if he moved forward a step his stare would be in her line of vision – if he moved backward he would lose his full view of her face. For a moment he had not realized how young she was. Now he remembered having seen her several times the year before – in bloomers.

Suddenly, involuntarily, he laughed, a short abrupt laugh – then, startled by himself, he turned and began to walk quickly away.

'Boy !'

Dexter stopped.

'Boy –'

Beyond question he was addressed. Not only that, but he was treated to that absurd smile, that preposterous smile – the memory of which at least a dozen men were to carry into middle age.

'Boy, do you know where the golf teacher is ?'

'He's giving a lesson.'

'Well, do you know where the caddy-master is?'

'He isn't here yet this morning.'

'Oh.' For a moment this baffled her. She stood alternately on her right and left foot.

'We'd like to get a caddy,' said the nurse. 'Mrs Mortimer Jones sent us out to play golf, and we don't know how without we get a caddy.'

Here she was stopped by an ominous glance from Miss Jones, followed immediately by the smile.

'There aren't any caddies here except me,' said Dexter to the nurse, 'and I got to stay here in charge until the caddy-master gets here.'

'Oh.'

Miss Jones and her retinue now withdrew, and at a proper distance from Dexter became involved in a heated conversation, which was concluded by Miss Jones taking one of the clubs and hitting it on the ground with violence. For further emphasis she raised it again and was about to bring it down smartly upon the nurse's bosom, when the nurse seized the club and twisted it from her hands.

'You damn little mean old thing!' cried Miss Jones wildly.

Another argument ensued. Realizing that the elements of the comedy were implied in the scene, Dexter several times began to laugh, but each time restrained the laugh before it reached audibility. He could not resist the monstrous conviction that the little girl was justified in beating the nurse.

The situation was resolved by the fortuitous appearance of the caddy-master, who was appealed to immediately by the nurse.

'Miss Jones is to have a little caddy, and this one says he can't go.'

'Mr McKenna said I was to wait here till you came,' said Dexter quickly.

'Well, he's here now.' Miss Jones smiled cheerfully at the caddy-master. Then she dropped her bag and set off at a haughty mince towards the first tee.

'Well?' The caddy-master turned to Dexter. 'What you standing there like a dummy for? Go pick up the young lady's clubs.'

'I don't think I'll go out today,' said Dexter.

'You don't –'

'I think I'll quit.'

The enormity of his decision frightened him. He was a favourite caddy, and the thirty dollars a month he earned through the summer were not to be made elsewhere around the lake. But he had received a strong emotional shock, and his perturbation required a violent and immediate outlet.

It is not so simple as that, either. As so frequently would be the case in the future, Dexter was unconsciously dictated to by his winter dreams.

2

Now, of course, the quality and the seasonability of these winter dreams varied, but the stuff of them remained. They persuaded Dexter several years later to pass up a business course at the State University – his father, prospering now, would have paid his way – for the precarious advantage of attending an older and more famous university in the East, where he was bothered by his scanty funds. But do not get the impression, because his winter dreams happened to be concerned at first with musings on the rich, that there was anything merely snobbish in the boy. He wanted not association with glittering things and glittering people – he wanted the glittering things themselves. Often he reached out for the best without knowing why he wanted it – and sometimes he ran up against the mysterious denials and prohibitions in which life indulges. It is with one of those denials and not with his career as a whole that this story deals.

He made money. It was rather amazing. After college he went to the city from which Black Bear Lake draws its wealthy patrons. When he was only twenty-three and had been there not quite two years, there were already people who liked to say: 'Now *there's* a boy —' All about him rich men's sons were peddling bonds precariously, or investing patrimonies precariously, or plodding through the two dozen volumes of the 'George Washington Commercial Course', but Dexter borrowed a thousand dollars on his college degree and his confident mouth, and bought a partnership in a laundry.

It was a small laundry when he went into it, but Dexter made a speciality of learning how the English washed fine woollen golf-stockings without shrinking them, and within a year he was catering to the trade that wore knickerbockers. Men were insisting that their Shetland hose and sweaters go to his laundry, just as they had insisted on a caddy who could find golf-balls. A little later he was doing their wives' lingerie as well – and running five branches in different parts of the city. Before he was twenty-seven he owned the largest string of laundries in his section of the country. It was then that he sold out and went to New York. But the part of his story that concerns us goes back to the days when he was making his first big success.

When he was twenty-three Mr Hart – one of the grey-haired men who like to say 'Now there's a boy' – gave him a guest card to the Sherry Island Golf Club for a weekend. So he signed his name one day on the register, and that afternoon played golf in a foursome with Mr Hart and Mr Sandwood and Mr T. A. Hedrick. He did not consider it necessary to remark that he had once carried Mr Hart's bag over this same links, and that he knew every trap and gully with his eyes shut – but he found himself glancing at the four caddies who trailed them, trying to catch a gleam or gesture that would remind him of himself, that would lessen the gap which lay between his present and his past.

It was a curious day, slashed abruptly with fleeting, familiar impressions. One minute he had the sense of being a trespasser – in the next he was impressed by the tremendous superiority he felt towards Mr T. A. Hedrick, who was a bore and not even a good golfer any more.

Then, because of a ball Mr Hart lost near the fifteenth green, an enormous thing happened. While they were searching the stiff grasses of the rough there was a clear call of 'Fore!' from behind a hill in their rear. And as they all turned abruptly from their search a bright new ball sliced abruptly over the hill and caught Mr T. A. Hedrick in the abdomen.

'By Gad!' cried Mr T. A. Hedrick, 'they ought to put some of these crazy women off the course. It's getting to be outrageous.'

A head and a voice came up together over the hill:

'Do you mind if we go through?'

'You hit me in the stomach!' declared Mr Hedrick wildly.

'Did I?' The girl approached the group of men. 'I'm sorry. I yelled "Fore!"'

Her glance fell casually on each of the men – then scanned the fairway for her ball.

'Did I bounce into the rough?'

It was impossible to determine whether this question was ingenuous or malicious. In a moment, however, she left no doubt, for as her partner came up over the hill she called cheerfully:

'Here I am! I'd have gone on the green except that I hit something.'

As she took her stance for a short mashie shot, Dexter looked at her closely. She wore a blue gingham dress, rimmed at throat and shoulders with a white edging that accentuated her tan. The quality of exaggeration, of thinness, which had made her passionate eyes and down-turning mouth absurd at eleven, was gone now. She was arrestingly beautiful. The colour in her cheeks was centred like the colour in a picture – it was not a 'high' colour, but a sort of fluctuating and feverish warmth, so shaded that it seemed at any moment it would recede and disappear. This colour and the mobility of her mouth gave a continual impression of flux, of intense life, of passionate vitality – balanced only partially by the sad luxury of her eyes.

She swung her mashie impatiently and without interest, pitching the ball into a sand-pit on the other side of the green.

With a quick, insincere smile and a careless 'Thank you!' she went on after it.

'That Judy Jones!' remarked Mr Hedrick on the next tee, as they waited – some moments – for her to play on ahead. 'All she needs is to be turned up and spanked for six months and then to be married off to an old-fashioned cavalry captain.'

'My God, she's good-looking!' said Mr Sandwood, who was just over thirty.

'Good-looking!' cried Mr Hedrick contemptuously, 'she always looks as if she wanted to be kissed! Turning those big cow-eyes on every calf in town!'

It was doubtful if Mr Hedrick intended a reference to the maternal instinct.

'She'd play pretty good golf if she'd try,' said Mr Sandwood.

'She has no form,' said Mr Hedrick solemnly.

'She has a nice figure,' said Mr Sandwood.

'Better thank the Lord she doesn't drive a swifter ball,' said Mr Hart, winking at Dexter.

Later in the afternoon the sun went down with a riotous swirl of gold and varying blues and scarlets, and left the dry, rustling night of Western summer. Dexter watched from the veranda of the Golf Club, watched the even overlap of the waters in the little wind, silver molasses under the harvest-moon. Then the moon held a finger to her lips and the lake became a clear pool, pale and quiet. Dexter put on his bathing-suit and swam out to the farthest raft, where he stretched dripping on the wet canvas of the springboard.

There was a fish jumping and a star shining and the lights around the lake were gleaming. Over on a dark peninsula a piano was playing the songs of last summer and of summers before that – songs from 'Chin-Chin' and 'The Count of Luxemburg' and 'The Chocolate Soldier' – and because the sound of a piano over a stretch of water had always seemed beautiful to Dexter he lay perfectly quiet and listened.

The tune the piano was playing at that moment had been gay and new five years before when Dexter was a sophomore at college. They had played it at a prom once when he could not afford the luxury of proms, and he had stood outside the gymnasium and listened. The sound of the tune precipitated in him a sort of ecstasy and it was with that ecstasy he viewed what happened to him now. It was a mood of intense appreciation, a sense that, for once, he was magnificently attuned to life and that everything about him was radiating a brightness and a glamour he might never know again.

A low, pale oblong detached itself suddenly from the darkness of the Island, spitting forth the reverberate sound of a racing motor-boat. Two white streamers of cleft water rolled themselves out behind it and almost immediately the boat was beside him, drowning out the hot tinkle of the piano in the drone of its spray. Dexter raising himself on his arms was aware of a figure standing at the wheel, of two dark eyes regarding him over the lengthening space of water – then the boat had gone by and was sweeping in an immense and purposeless circle of spray round and round in the middle of the lake. With equal eccentricity one of the circles flattened out and headed back towards the raft.

'Who's that?' she called, shutting off her motor. She was so near now that Dexter could see her bathing-suit, which consisted apparently of pink rompers.

The nose of the boat bumped the raft, and as the latter tilted rakishly he was precipitated toward her. With different degrees of interest they recognized each other.

'Aren't you one of those men we played through this afternoon,' she demanded.

He was.

'Well, do you know how to drive a motor-boat? Because if you do I wish you'd drive this one so I can ride on the surfboard behind. My name is Judy Jones' – she favoured him with an absurd smirk – rather, what tried to be a smirk, for, twist her mouth as she might, it was not grotesque, it was merely beautiful – 'and I live in a house over there on the Island, and in that house there is a man waiting for me. When he drove up at the door I drove out of the dock because he says I'm his ideal.'

There was a fish jumping and a star shining and the lights around the lake were gleaming. Dexter sat beside Judy Jones and she explained how her boat was driven. Then she was in the water, swimming to the floating surf-board with a sinuous crawl. Watching her was without effort to the eye, watching a branch waving or a sea-gull flying. Her arms, burned to butter-nut, moved sinuously among the dull platinum ripples, elbow appearing first, casting the forearm back with a cadence of falling water, then reaching out and down, stabbing a path ahead.

They moved out into the lake; turning, Dexter saw that she was kneeling on the low rear of the now up-tilted surf-board.

'Go faster,' she called, 'fast as it'll go.'

Obediently he jammed the lever forward and the white spray mounted at the bow. When he looked around again the girl was standing up on the rushing board, her arms spread wide, her eyes lifted towards the moon.

'It's awful cold,' she shouted. 'What's your name?'

He told her.

'Well, why don't you come to dinner tomorrow night?'

His heart turned over like the fly-wheel of the boat, and, for the second time, her casual whim gave a new direction to his life.

3

Next evening while he waited for her to come downstairs, Dexter peopled the soft deep summer room and the sun-porch that opened from it with the men who had already loved Judy Jones. He knew the sort of men they were – the men who when he first went to college had entered from the great prep schools with graceful clothes and the deep tan of healthy summers. He had seen that, in one sense, he was better than these men. He was newer and stronger. Yet in acknowledging to himself that he wished his children to be like them he was admitting that he was but the rough, strong stuff from which they eternally sprang.

When the time had come for him to wear good clothes, he had known who were the best tailors in America, and the best tailors in America had made him the suit he wore this evening. He had acquired that particular reserve peculiar to his university, that set it off from other universities. He recognized the value to him of such a mannerism and he had adopted it; he knew that to be careless in dress and manner required more confidence than to be careful. But carelessness was for his children. His mother's name had been Krimslich. She was a Bohemian of the peasant class and she had talked broken English to the end of her days. Her son must keep to the set patterns.

At a little after seven Judy Jones came downstairs. She wore a blue silk afternoon dress, and he was disappointed at first that she had not put on something more elaborate. This feeling was accentuated when, after a brief greeting, she went to the door of a butler's pantry and pushing it open called: 'You can serve dinner, Martha.' He had rather expected that a butler would announce dinner, that there would be a cocktail. Then he put these thoughts behind him as they sat down side by side on a lounge and looked at each other.

'Father and mother won't be here,' she said thoughtfully.

He remembered the last time he had seen her father, and he was glad the parents were not to be here tonight – they might wonder who he was. He had been born in Keeble, a Minnesota village fifty miles farther north, and he always gave Keeble as his home instead of Black Bear Village. Country towns were well enough to come from if they weren't inconveniently in sight and used as foot-stools by fashionable lakes.

They talked of his university, which she had visited frequently during the past two years, and of the nearby city which supplied Sherry Island with its patrons, and whither Dexter would return next day to his prospering laundries.

During dinner she slipped into a moody depression which gave Dexter a feeling of uneasiness. Whatever petulance she uttered in her throaty voice worried him. Whatever she smiled at, at him, at a chicken liver, at nothing – it disturbed him that her smile could have no root in mirth, or even in amusement. When the scarlet corners of her lips turned down, it was less a smile than an invitation to a kiss.

Then, after dinner, she led him out on the dark sun-porch and deliberately changed the atmosphere.

'Do you mind if I weep a little?' she said.

'I'm afraid I'm boring you,' he responded quickly.

'You're not. I like you. But I've just had a terrible afternoon. There was a man I cared about, and this afternoon he told me out of a clear sky that he was poor as a church-mouse. He'd never even hinted it before. Does this sound horribly mundane?'

'Perhaps he was afraid to tell you.'

'Suppose he was,' she answered. 'He didn't start right. You see, if I'd thought of him as poor – well, I've been mad about loads of poor men, and fully intended to marry them all. But in this case, I hadn't thought of him that way, and my interest in him wasn't strong enough to survive the shock. As if a girl calmly informed her fiancé that she was a widow. He might not object to widows, but –

'Let's start right,' she interrupted herself suddenly. 'Who are you, anyhow?'

For a moment Dexter hesitated. Then:

'I'm nobody,' he announced. 'My career is largely a matter of futures.'

'Are you poor?'

'No,' he said frankly, 'I'm probably making more money than any man my age in the Northwest. I know that's an obnoxious remark, but you advised me to start right.'

There was a pause. Then she smiled and the corners of her mouth drooped and an almost imperceptible sway brought her closer to him, looking up into his eyes. A lump rose in Dexter's throat, and he waited breathless for the experiment, facing the unpredictable compound that would form mysteriously from the elements of their lips. Then he saw – she communicated her excitement to him, lavishly, deeply, with kisses that were not a promise but a fulfilment. They aroused in him not hunger de-

manding renewal but surfeit that would demand more surfeit
. . . kisses that were like charity, creating want by holding back
nothing at all.

It did not take him many hours to decide that he had wanted
Judy Jones ever since he was a proud, desirous little boy.

4

It began like that – and continued, with varying shades of
intensity, on such a note right up to the dénouement. Dexter
surrendered a part of himself to the most direct and un-
principled personality with which he had ever come in contact.
Whatever Judy wanted, she went after with the full pressure
of her charm. There was no divergence of method, no jockey-
ing for position or premeditation of effects – there was a very
little mental side to any of her affairs. She simply made men
conscious to the highest degree of her physical loveliness.
Dexter had no desire to change her. Her deficiencies were knit
up with a passionate energy that transcended and justified
them.

When, as Judy's head lay against his shoulder that first night,
she whispered, 'I don't know what's the matter with me. Last
night I thought I was in love with a man and tonight I think I'm
in love with you –', it seemed to him a beautiful and romantic
thing to say. It was the exquisite excitability that for the
moment he controlled and owned. But a week later he was
compelled to view this same quality in a different light. She
took him in her roadster to a picnic supper, and after supper she
disappeared, likewise in her roadster, with another man. Dexter became enormously upset and was scarcely able to be
decently civil to the other people present. When she assured
him that she had not kissed the other man, he knew she was
lying – yet he was glad that she had taken the trouble to lie to
him.

He was, as he found before the summer ended, one of a varying dozen who circulated about her. Each of them had at one
time been favoured above all others – about half of them still

basked in the solace of occasional sentimental revivals. Whenever one showed signs of dropping out through long neglect, she granted him a brief honeyed hour; which encouraged him to tag along for a year or so longer. Judy made these forays upon the helpless and defeated without malice, indeed half unconscious that there was anything mischievous in what she did.

When a new man came to town everyone dropped out — dates were automatically cancelled.

The helpless part of trying to do anything about it was that she did it all herself. She was not a girl who could be 'won' in the kinetic sense — she was proof against cleverness, she was proof against charm; if any of these assailed her too strongly she would immediately resolve the affair to a physical basis, and under the magic of her physical splendour the strong as well as the brilliant played her game and not their own. She was entertained only by the gratification of her desires and by the direct exercise of her own charm. Perhaps from so much youthful love, so many youthful lovers, she had come, in self-defence, to nourish herself wholly from within.

Succeeding Dexter's first exhilaration came restlessness and dissatisfaction. The helpless ecstasy of losing himself in her was opiate rather than tonic. It was fortunate for his work during the winter that those moments of ecstasy came infrequently. Early in their acquaintance it had seemed for a while that there was a deep and spontaneous mutual attraction — that first August, for example, three days of long evenings on her dusky veranda, of strange wan kisses through the late afternoon, in shadowy alcoves or behind the protecting trellises of the garden arbours, of mornings when she was fresh as a dream and almost shy at meeting him in the clarity of the rising day. There was all the ecstasy of an engagement about it, sharpened by his realization that there was no engagement. It was during those three days that, for the first time, he had asked her to marry him. She said 'maybe some day', she said 'kiss me', she said 'I'd like to marry you', she said 'I love you' — she said — nothing.

The three days were interrupted by the arrival of a New York man who visited at her house for half September. To Dexter's agony, rumour engaged them. The man was the son of the president of a great trust company. But at the end of a month it was reported that Judy was yawning. At a dance one night she sat all evening in a motor-boat with a local beau, while the New Yorker searched the club for her frantically. She told the local beau that she was bored with her visitor, and two days later he left. She was seen with him at the station, and it was reported that he looked very mournful indeed.

On this note the summer ended. Dexter was twenty-four, and he found himself increasingly in a position to do as he wished. He joined two clubs in the city and lived at one of them. Though he was by no means an integral part of the stag-lines at these clubs, he managed to be on hand at dances where Judy Jones was likely to appear. He could have gone out socially as much as he liked – he was an eligible young man, now, and popular with down-town fathers. His confessed devotion to Judy Jones had rather solidified his position. But he had no social aspirations and rather despised the dancing men who were always on tap for the Thursday or Saturday parties and who filled in at dinners with the younger married set. Already he was playing with the idea of going East to New York. He wanted to take Judy Jones with him. No disillusion as to the world in which she had grown up could cure his illusion as to her desirability.

Remember that – for only in the light of it can what he did for her be understood.

Eighteen months after he first met Judy Jones he became engaged to another girl. Her name was Irene Scheerer, and her father was one of the men who had always believed in Dexter. Irene was light-haired and sweet and honourable, and a little stout, and she had two suitors whom she pleasantly relinquished when Dexter formally asked her to marry him.

Summer, fall, winter, spring, another summer, another fall – so much he had given of his active life to the incorrigible lips of Judy Jones. She had treated him with interest, with encouragement, with malice, with indifference, with contempt. She had inflicted on him the innumerable little slights and indignities possible in such a case – as if in revenge for having ever cared for him at all. She had beckoned him and yawned at him and beckoned him again and he had responded often with bitterness and narrowed eyes. She had brought him ecstatic happiness and intolerable agony of spirit. She had caused him untold inconvenience and not a little trouble. She had insulted him, and she had ridden over him, and she had played his interest in her against his interest in his work – for fun. She had done everything to him except to criticise him – this she had not done – it seemed to him only because it might have sullied the utter indifference she manifested and sincerely felt towards him.

When autumn had come and gone again it occurred to him that he could not have Judy Jones. He had to beat this into his mind but he convinced himself at last. He lay awake at night for a while and argued it over. He told himself the trouble and the pain she had caused him, he enumerated her glaring deficiencies as a wife. Then he said to himself that he loved her, and after a while he fell asleep. For a week, lest he imagined her husky voice over the telephone or her eyes opposite him at lunch, he worked hard and late, and at night he went to his office and plotted out his years.

At the end of a week he went to a dance and cut in on her once. For almost the first time since they had met he did not ask her to sit out with him or tell her that she was lovely. It hurt him that she did not miss these things – that was all. He was not jealous when he saw that there was a new man tonight. He had been hardened against jealousy long before.

He stayed late at the dance. He sat for an hour with Irene Scheerer and talked about books and about music. He knew very little about either. But he was beginning to be master of his own time now, and he had a rather priggish notion that he – the young and already fabulously successful Dexter Green – should know more about such things.

That was in October, when he was twenty-five. In January,

Dexter and Irene became engaged. It was to be announced in June, and they were to be married three months later.

The Minnesota winter prolonged itself interminably, and it was almost May when the winds came soft and the snow ran down into Black Bear Lake at last. For the first time in over a year Dexter was enjoying a certain tranquillity of spirit. Judy Jones had been in Florida, and afterwards in Hot Springs, and somewhere she had been engaged, and somewhere she had broken it off. At first, when Dexter had definitely given her up, it had made him sad that people still linked them together and asked for news of her, but when he began to be placed at dinner next to Irene Scheerer people didn't ask him about her any more – they told him about her. He ceased to be an authority on her.

May at last. Dexter walked the streets at night when the darkness was damp as rain, wondering that so soon, with so little done, so much of ecstasy had gone from him. May one year back had been marked by Judy's poignant, unforgivable, yet forgiven turbulence – it had been one of those rare times when he fancied she had grown to care for him. That old penny's worth of happiness he had spent for this bushel of content. He knew that Irene would be no more than a curtain spread behind him, a hand moving among gleaming teacups, a voice calling to children ... fire and loveliness were gone, the magic of nights and the wonder of the varying hours and seasons ... slender lips, down-turning, dropping to his lips and bearing him up into a heaven of eyes.... The thing was deep in him. He was too strong and alive for it to die lightly.

In the middle of May when the weather balanced for a few days on the thin bridge that led to deep summer he turned in one night at Irene's house. Their engagement was to be announced in a week now – no one would be surprised at it. And tonight they would sit together on the lounge at the University Club and look on for an hour at the dancers. It gave him a sense of solidity to go with her – she was so sturdily popular, so intensely 'great'.

He mounted the steps of the brownstone house and stepped inside.

'Irene,' he called.

Mrs Scheerer came out of the living-room to meet him.

'Dexter,' she said, 'Irene's gone upstairs with a splitting headache. She wanted to go with you but I made her go to bed.'

'Nothing serious, I –'

'Oh, no. She's going to play golf with you in the morning. You can spare her for just one night, can't you, Dexter?'

Her smile was kind. She and Dexter liked each other. In the living-room he talked for a moment before he said good night.

Returning to the University Club, where he had rooms, he stood in the doorway for a moment and watched the dancers. He leaned against the door-post, nodded at a man or two – yawned.

'Hello, darling.'

The familiar voice at his elbow startled him. Judy Jones had left a man and crossed the room to him – Judy Jones, a slender enamelled doll in cloth of gold: gold in a band at her head, gold in two slipper points at her dress's hem. The fragile glow of her face seemed to blossom as she smiled at him. A breeze of warmth and light blew through the room. His hands in the pockets of his dinner-jacket tightened spasmodically. He was filled with a sudden excitement.

'When did you get back?' he asked casually.

'Come here and I'll tell you about it.'

She turned and he followed her. She had been away – he could have wept at the wonder of her return. She had passed through enchanted streets, doing things that were like provocative music. All mysterious happenings, all fresh and quickening hopes, had gone away with her, come back with her now.

She turned in the doorway.

'Have you a car here? If you haven't, I have.'

'I have a coupé.'

In then, with a rustle of golden cloth. He slammed the door. Into so many cars she had stepped – like this – like that – her back against the leather, so – her elbow resting on the door – waiting. She would have been soiled long since had there been anything to soil her – except herself – but this was her own self outpouring.

With an effort he forced himself to start the car and back into the street. This was nothing, he must remember. She had done this before, and he had put her behind him, as he would have crossed a bad account from his books.

He drove slowly down-town and, affecting abstraction, traversed the deserted streets of the business section, peopled here and there where a movie was giving out its crowd or where consumptive or pugilistic youth lounged in front of pool halls. The clink of glasses and the slap of hands on the bars issued from saloons, cloisters of glazed glass and dirty yellow light.

She was watching him closely and the silence was embarrassing, yet in this crisis he could find no casual word with which to profane the hour. At a convenient turning he began to zigzag back towards the University Club.

'Have you missed me?' she asked suddenly.

'Everybody missed you.'

He wondered if she knew of Irene Scheerer. She had been back only a day – her absence had been almost contemporaneous with his engagement.

'What a remark!' Judy laughed sadly – without sadness. She looked at him searchingly. He became absorbed in the dashboard.

'You're handsomer than you used to be,' she said thoughtfully. 'Dexter, you have the most rememberable eyes.'

He could have laughed at this, but he did not laugh. It was the sort of thing that was said to sophormores. Yet it stabbed at him.

'I'm awfully tired of everything, darling.' She called everyone darling, endowing the endearment with careless, individual cameraderie. 'I wish you'd marry me.'

The directness of this confused him. He should have told her now that he was going to marry another girl, but he could not tell her. He could as easily have sworn that he had never loved her.

'I think we'd get along,' she continued, on the same note, 'unless probably you've forgotten me and fallen in love with another girl.'

Her confidence was obviously enormous. She had said, in effect, that she found such a thing impossible to believe, that if it were true he had merely committed a childish indiscretion – and probably to show off. She would forgive him, because it was not a matter of any moment but rather something to be brushed aside lightly.

'Of course you could never love anybody but me,' she continued, 'I like the way you love me. Oh, Dexter, have you forgotten last year?'

'No, I haven't forgotten.'

'Neither have I!'

Was she sincerely moved – or was she carried along by the wave of her own acting?

'I wish we could be like that again,' she said, and he forced himself to answer :

'I don't think we can.'

'I suppose not.... I hear you're giving Irene Scheerer a violent rush.'

There was not the faintest emphasis on the name, yet Dexter was suddenly ashamed.

'Oh, take me home,' cried Judy suddenly; 'I don't want to go back to that idiotic dance – with those children.'

Then, as he turned up the street that led to the residence district, Judy began to cry quietly to herself. He had never seen her cry before.

The dark street lightened, the dwellings of the rich loomed up around them, he stopped his coupé in front of the great white bulk of the Mortimer Joneses' house, somnolent, gorgeous, drenched with the splendour of the damp moonlight. Its solidity startled him. The strong walls, the steel of the girders, the breadth and beam and pomp of it were there only to bring out the contrast with the young beauty beside him. It was sturdy to accentuate her slightness – as if to show what a breeze could be generated by a butterfly's wing.

He sat perfectly quiet, his nerves in wild clamour, afraid that if he moved he would find her irresistibly in his arms. Two tears had rolled down her wet face and trembled on her upper lip.

'I'm more beautiful than anybody else,' she said brokenly, 'why can't I be happy?' Her moist eyes tore at his stability – her mouth turned slowly downwards with an exquisite sadness: 'I'd like to marry you if you'll have me, Dexter. I suppose you think I'm not worth having, but I'll be so beautiful for you, Dexter.'

A million phrases of anger, pride, passion, hatred, tenderness fought on his lips. Then a perfect wave of emotion washed over him, carrying off with it a sediment of wisdom, of convention, of doubt, of honour. This was his girl who was speaking, his own, his beautiful, his pride.

'Won't you come in?' He heard her draw in her breath sharply.

Waiting.

'All right,' his voice was trembling, 'I'll come in.'

5

It was strange that neither when it was over nor a long time afterwards did he regret that night. Looking at it from the perspective of ten years, the fact that Judy's flare for him endured just one month seemed of little importance. Nor did it matter that by his yielding he subjected himself to a deeper agony in the end and gave serious hurt to Irene Scheerer and to Irene's parents, who had befriended him. There was nothing sufficiently pictorial about Irene's grief to stamp itself on his mind.

Dexter was at bottom hard-minded. The attitude of the city on his action was of no importance to him, not because he was going to leave the city, but because any outside attitude on the situation seemed superficial. He was completely indifferent to popular opinion. Nor, when he had seen that it was no use, that he did not possess in himself the power to move fundamentally or to hold Judy Jones, did he bear any malice towards her. He loved her, and he would love her until the day he was too old for loving – but he could not have her. So he tasted the deep pain that is reserved only for the strong, just as he had tasted for a little while the deep happiness.

Even the ultimate falsity of the grounds upon which Judy terminated the engagement: that she did not want to 'take him away' from Irene – Judy who had wanted nothing else – did not revolt him. He was beyond any revulsion or any amusement.

He went East in February with the intention of selling out his laundries and settling in New York – but the war came to America in March and changed his plans. He returned to the West, handed over the management of the business to his partner, and went into the first officers' training-camp in late April. He was one of those young thousands who greeted the war with a certain amount of relief, welcoming the liberation from webs of tangled emotion.

6

This story is not his biography, remember, although things creep into it which have nothing to do with those dreams he had when he was young. We are almost done with them and with him now. There is only one more incident to be related here, and it happens seven years farther on.

It took place in New York, where he had done well – so well that there were no barriers too high for him. He was thirty-two years old, and, except for one flying trip immediately after the war, he had not been West in seven years. A man named Devlin from Detroit came into his office to see him in a business way, and then and there this incident occurred, and closed out, so to speak, this particular side of his life.

'So you're from the Middle West,' said the man Devlin with careless curiosity. 'That's funny – I thought men like you were probably born and raised on Wall Street. You know – wife of one of my best friends in Detroit came from your city. I was an usher at the wedding.'

Dexter waited with no apprehension of what was coming.

'Judy Simms,' said Devlin with no particular interest; 'Judy Jones she was once.'

'Yes, I knew her.' A dull impatience spread over him. He had heard, of course, that she was married – perhaps deliberately he had heard no more.

'Awfully nice girl,' brooded Devlin meaninglessly, 'I'm sort of sorry for her.'

'Why?' Something in Dexter was alert, receptive, at once.

'Oh, Lud Simms has gone to pieces in a way. I don't mean he ill-uses her, but he drinks and runs around –'

'Doesn't she run around?'

'No. Stays at home with her kids.'

'Oh.'

'She's a little too old for him,' said Devlin.

'Too old!' cried Dexter. 'Why, man, she's only twenty-seven.'

He was possessed with a wild notion of rushing out into the streets and taking a train to Detroit. He rose to his feet spasmodically.

'I guess you're busy,' Devlin apologized quickly. 'I didn't realize –'

'No, I'm not busy,' said Dexter, steadying his voice. 'I'm not busy at all. Not busy at all. Did you say she was – twenty-seven? No, I said she was twenty-seven.'

'Yes, you did,' agreed Devlin dryly.

'Go on, then. Go on.'

'What do you mean?'

'About Judy Jones.'

Devlin looked at him helplessly.

'Well, that's – I told you all there is to it. He treats her like the devil. Oh, they're not going to get divorced or anything. When he's particularly outrageous she forgives him. In fact, I'm inclined to think she loves him. She was a pretty girl when she first came to Detroit.'

A pretty girl! The phrase struck Dexter as ludicrous.

'Isn't she – a pretty girl, any more?'

'Oh, she's all right.'

'Look here,' said Dexter, sitting down suddenly. 'I don't understand. You say she was a "pretty girl" and now you say she's "all right". I don't understand what you mean – Judy Jones wasn't a pretty girl, at all. She was a great beauty. Why, I knew her, I knew her. She was –'

Devlin laughed pleasantly.

'I'm not trying to start a row,' he said. 'I think Judy's a nice girl and I like her. I can't understand how a man like Lud Simms could fall madly in love with her, but he did.' Then he added: 'Most of the women like her.'

Dexter looked closely at Devlin, thinking wildly that there must be a reason for this, some insensitivity in the man or some private malice.

'Lots of women fade just like *that*,' Devlin snapped his fingers. 'You must have seen it happen. Perhaps I've forgotten how pretty she was at her wedding. I've seen her so much since then, you see. She has nice eyes.'

A sort of dullness settled down upon Dexter. For the first time in his life he felt like getting very drunk. He knew that he was laughing loudly at something Devlin had said, but he did not know what it was or why it was funny. When, in a few minutes, Devlin went he lay down on his lounge and looked out of the window at the New York sky-line into which the sun was sinking in dull lovely shades of pink and gold.

He had thought that having nothing else to lose he was invulnerable at last – but he knew that he had just lost something more, as surely as if he had married Judy Jones and seen her fade away before his eyes.

The dream was gone. Something had been taken from him. In a sort of panic he pushed the palms of his hands into his eyes and tried to bring up a picture of the waters lapping on Sherry Island and the moonlit veranda, and gingham on the golf-links and the dry sun and the gold colour of her neck's soft down. And her mouth damp to his kisses and her eyes plaintive with melancholy and her freshness like new fine linen in the morning. Why, these things were no longer in the world! They had existed and they existed no longer.

For the first time in years the tears were streaming down his face. But they were for himself now. He did not care about mouth and eyes and moving hands. He wanted to care, and he could not care. For he had gone away and he could never go back any more. The gates were closed, the sun was gone down, and there was no beauty but the grey beauty of steel that withstands all time. Even the grief he could have borne was left behind in the country of illusion, of youth, of the richness of life, where his winter dreams had flourished.

'Long ago,' he said, 'long ago, there was something in me, but now that thing is gone. Now that thing is gone, that thing is gone. I cannot cry. I cannot care. That thing will come back no more.'

'The Sensible Thing'

I

At the Great American Lunch Hour young George O'Kelly straightened his desk deliberately and with an assumed air of interest. No one in the office must know that he was in a hurry, for success is a matter of atmosphere, and it is not well to advertise the fact that your mind is separated from your work by a distance of seven hundred miles.

But once out of the building he set his teeth and began to run, glancing now and then at the gay noon of early spring which filled Times Square and loitered less than twenty feet over the heads of the crowd. The crowd all looked slightly upwards and took deep March breaths, and the sun dazzled their eyes so that scarcely anyone saw anyone else but only their own reflection on the sky.

George O'Kelly, whose mind was over seven hundred miles away, thought that all outdoors was horrible. He rushed into the subway, and for ninety-five blocks bent a frenzied glance on a car-card which showed vividly how he had only one chance in five of keeping his teeth for ten years. At 137th Street he broke off his study of commercial art, left the subway, and began to run again, a tireless, anxious run that brought him this time to his home – one room in a high, horrible apartment-house in the middle of nowhere.

There it was on the bureau, the letter – in sacred ink, on blessed paper – all over the city, people, if they listened, could hear the beating of George O'Kelly's heart. He read the commas, the blots, and the thumb-smudge on the margin – then he threw himself hopelessly upon his bed.

He was in a mess, one of those terrific messes which are ordinary incidents in the life of the poor, which follow poverty like birds of prey. The poor go under or go up or go wrong or even go on, somehow, in a way the poor have – but George O'Kelly was so new to poverty that had any one denied the uniqueness of his case he would have been astounded.

Less than two years ago he had been graduated with honours from The Massachusetts Institute of Technology and had taken a position with a firm of construction engineers in southern Tennessee. All his life he had thought in terms of tunnels and skyscrapers and great squat dams and tall, three-towered bridges, that were like dancers holding hands in a row, with heads as tall as cities and skirts of cable strand. It had seemed romantic to George O'Kelly to change the sweep of rivers and the shape of mountains so that life could flourish in the old bad lands of the world where it had never taken root before. He loved steel, and there was always steel near him in his dreams, liquid steel, steel in bars, and blocks and beams and formless plastic masses, waiting for him, as paint and canvas to his hand. Steel inexhaustible, to be made lovely and austere in his imaginative fire . . .

At present he was an insurance clerk at forty dollars a week with his dream slipping fast behind him. The dark little girl who had made this mess, this terrible and intolerable mess, was waiting to be sent for in a town in Tennessee.

In fifteen minutes the woman from whom he sublet his room knocked and asked him with maddening kindness if, since he was home, he would have some lunch. He shook his head, but the interruption aroused him, and getting up from the bed he wrote a telegram.

'Letter depressed me have you lost your nerve you are foolish and just upset to think of breaking off why not marry me immediately sure we can make it all right –'

He hesitated for a wild minute, and then added in a hand that could scarcely be recognized as his own: 'In any case I will arrive tomorrow at six o'clock.'

When he finished he ran out of the apartment and down to the telegraph office near the subway stop. He possessed in this world not quite one hundred dollars, but the letter showed that she was 'nervous' and this left him no choice. He knew what 'nervous' meant – that she was emotionally depressed, that the prospect of marrying into a life of poverty and struggle was putting too much strain upon her love.

George O'Kelly reached the insurance company at his usual run, the run that had become almost second nature to him, that seemed best to express the tension under which he lived. He went straight to the manager's office.

'I want to see you, Mr Chambers,' he announced breathlessly.

'Well?' Two eyes, eyes like winter windows, glared at him with ruthless impersonality.

'I want to get four days' vacation.'

'Why, you had a vacation just two weeks ago!' said Mr Chambers in surprise.

'That's true,' admitted the distraught young man, 'but now I've got to have another.'

'Where'd you go last time? To your home?'

'No, I went to – a place in Tennessee.'

'Well, where do you want to go this time?'

'Well, this time I want to go to – a place in Tennessee.'

'You're consistent, anyhow,' said the manager dryly. 'But I didn't realize you were employed here as a travelling salesman.'

'I'm not,' cried George desperately, 'but I've got to go.'

'All right,' agreed Mr Chambers ,'but you don't have to come back. So don't!'

'I won't.' And to his own astonishment as well as Mr Chambers' George's face grew pink with pleasure. He felt happy, exultant – for the first time in six months he was absolutely free. Tears of gratitude stood in his eyes, and he seized Mr Chambers warmly by the hand.

'I want to thank you,' he said with a rush of emotion, 'I don't want to come back. I think I'd have gone crazy if you'd said that I could come back. Only I couldn't quit myself, you see, and I want to thank you for – for quitting for me.'

He waved his hand magnanimously, shouted aloud, 'You owe

me three days' salary but you can keep it!' and rushed from the office. Mr Chambers rang for his stenographer to ask if O'Kelly had seemed queer lately. He had fired many men in the course of his career, and they had taken it in many different ways, but none of them had thanked him – ever before.

2

Jonquil Cary was her name, and to George O'Kelly nothing had ever looked so fresh and pale as her face when she saw him and fled to him eagerly along the station platform. Her arms were raised to him, her mouth was half parted for his kiss, when she held him off suddenly and lightly and, with a touch of embarrassment, looked around. Two boys, somewhat younger than George, were standing in the background.

'This is Mr Craddock and Mr Holt,' she announced cheerfully. 'You met them when you were here before.'

Disturbed by the transition of a kiss into an introduction and suspecting some hidden significance, George was more confused when he found that the automobile which was to carry them to Jonquil's house belonged to one of the two young men. It seemed to put him at a disadvantage. On the way Jonquil chattered between the front and back seats, and when he tried to slip his arm around her under cover of the twilight she compelled him with a quick movement to take her hand instead.

'Is this street on the way to your house?' he whispered. 'I don't recognize it.'

'It's the new boulevard. Jerry just got this car today, and he wants to show it to me before he takes us home.'

When, after twenty minutes, they were deposited at Jonquil's house, George felt that the first happiness of the meeting, the joy he had recognized so surely in her eyes back in the station, had been dissipated by the intrusion of the ride. Something that he had looked forward to had been rather casually lost, and he was brooding on this as he said good night stiffly to the two young men. Then his ill-humour faded as Jonquil drew him into a familiar embrace under the dim light of the front hall and told him in a dozen ways, of which the best was without words, how she had missed him. Her emotion reassured him, promised his anxious heart that everything would be all right.

They sat together on the sofa, overcome by each other's presence, beyond all except fragmentary endearments. At the supper hour Jonquil's father and mother appeared and were glad to see George. They liked him, and had been interested in his engineering career when he had first come to Tennessee over a year before. They had been sorry when he had given it up and gone to New York to look for something more immediately profitable, but while they deplored the curtailment of his career they sympathized with him and were ready to recognize the engagement. During dinner they asked about his progress in New York.

'Everything's going fine,' he told them with enthusiasm. 'I've been promoted – better salary.'

He was miserable as he said this – but they were all *so* glad.

'They must like you,' said Mrs Cary, 'that's certain – or they wouldn't let you off twice in three weeks to come down here.'

'I told them they had to,' explained George hastily; 'I told them if they didn't I wouldn't work for them any more.'

'But you ought to save your money,' Mrs Cary reproached him gently. 'Not spend it all on this expensive trip.'

Dinner was over – he and Jonquil were alone and she came back into his arms.

'So glad you're here,' she sighed. 'Wish you never were going away again, darling.'

'Do you miss me?'

'Oh, so much, so much.'

'Do you – do other men come to see you often? Like those two kids?'

The question surprised her. The dark velvet eyes stared at him.

'Why, of course they do. All the time. Why – I've told you in letters that they did, dearest.'

This was true – when he had first come to the city there had been already a dozen boys around her, responding to her picturesque fragility with adolescent worship, and a few of them perceiving that her beautiful eyes were also sane and kind.

'Do you expect me never to go anywhere' – Jonquil demanded, leaning back against the sofa-pillows until she seemed to look at him from many miles away – 'and just fold my hands and sit still – forever?'

'What do you mean?' he blurted out in a panic. 'Do you mean you think I'll never have enough money to marry you?'

'Oh, don't jump at conclusions so, George.'

'I'm not jumping at conclusions. That's what you said.'

George decided suddenly that he was on dangerous grounds. He had not intended to let anything spoil this night. He tried to take her again in his arms, but she resisted unexpectedly, saying:

'It's hot. I'm going to get the electric fan.'

When the fan was adjusted they sat down again, but he was in a supersensitive mood and involuntarily he plunged into the specific world he had intended to avoid.

'When will you marry me?'

'Are you ready for me to marry you?'

All at once his nerves gave way, and he sprang to his feet.

'Let's shut off that damned fan,' he cried, 'it drives me wild. It's like a clock ticking away all the time I'll be with you. I came here to be happy and forget everything about New York and time –'

He sank down on the sofa as suddenly as he had risen. Jonquil turned off the fan, and drawing his head down into her lap began stroking his hair.

'Let's sit like this,' she said softly, 'just sit quiet like this, and I'll put you to sleep. You're all tired and nervous and your sweetheart'll take care of you.'

'But I don't want to sit like this,' he complained, jerking up suddenly, 'I don't want to sit like this at all. I want you to kiss me. That's the only thing that makes me rest. And any ways I'm not nervous – it's you that's nervous. I'm not nervous at all.'

To prove that he wasn't nervous he left the couch and plumped himself into a rocking-chair across the room.

'Just when I'm ready to marry you you write me the most nervous letters, as if you're going to back out, and I have to come rushing down here – '

'You don't have to come if you don't want to.'

'But I *do* want to!' insisted George.

It seemed to him that he was being very cool and logical and that she was putting him deliberately in the wrong. With every word they were drawing farther and farther apart – and he was unable to stop himself or to keep worry and pain out of his voice.

But in a minute Jonquil began to cry sorrowfully and he came back to the sofa and put his arm around her. He was the comforter now, drawing her head close to his shoulder, murmuring old familiar things until she grew calmer and only trembled a little, spasmodically, in his arms. For over an hour they sat there, while the evening pianos thumped their last cadences into the street outside. George did not move, or think, or hope, lulled into numbness by the premonition of disaster. The clock would tick on, past eleven, past twelve, and then Mrs Cary would call down gently over the banister – beyond that he saw only tomorrow and despair.

3

In the heat of the next day the breaking-point came. They had each guessed the truth about the other, but of the two she was the more ready to admit the situation.

'There's no use going on,' she said miserably, 'you know you hate the insurance business, and you'll never do well in it.'

'That's not it,' he insisted stubbornly; 'I hate going on alone. If you'll marry me and come with me and take a chance with me, I can make good at anything, but not while I'm worrying about you down here.'

She was silent a long time before she answered, not thinking – for she had seen the end – but only waiting, because she knew that every word would seem more cruel than the last. Finally she spoke :

'George, I love you with all my heart, and I don't see how I can ever love anyone else but you. If you'd been ready for me two months ago I'd have married you – now I can't because it doesn't seem to be the sensible thing.'

He made wild accusations – there was someone else – she was keeping something from him !

'No, there's no one else.'

This was true. But reacting from the strain of this affair she had found relief in the company of young boys like Jerry Holt, who had the merit of meaning absolutely nothing in her life.

George didn't take the situation well, at all. He seized her in his arms and tried literally to kiss her into marrying him at once. When this failed, he broke into a long monologue of self-pity, and ceased only when he saw that he was making himself despicable in her sight. He threatened to leave when he had no intention of leaving, and refused to go when she told him that, after all, it was best that he should.

For a while she was sorry, then for another while she was merely kind.

'You'd better go now,' she cried at last, so loud that Mrs Cary came downstairs in alarm.

'Is something the matter ?'

'I'm going away, Mrs Cary,' said George brokenly. Jonquil had left the room.

'Don't feel so badly, George.' Mrs Cary blinked at him in helpless sympathy – sorry and, in the same breath, glad that the little tragedy was almost done. 'If I were you I'd go home to your mother for a week or so. Perhaps after all this is the sensible thing –'

'Please don't talk,' he cried. 'Please don't say anything to me now ! '

Jonquil came into the room again, her sorrow and her nervousness alike tucked under powder and rouge and hat.

'I've ordered a taxicab,' she said impersonally. 'We can drive around until your train leaves.'

She walked out on the front porch. George put on his coat and hat and stood for a minute exhausted in the hall – he had eaten scarcely a bite since he had left New York. Mrs Cary came over, drew his head down and kissed him on the cheek, and he felt very ridiculous and weak in his knowledge that the scene had been ridiculous and weak at the end. If he had only gone the night before – left her for the last time with a decent pride.

The taxi had come, and for an hour these two that had been lovers rode along the less-frequented streets. He held her hand and grew calmer in the sunshine, seeing too late that there had been nothing all along to do or say.

'I'll come back,' he told her.

'I know you will,' she answered, trying to put a cheery faith into her voice. 'And we'll write each other – sometimes.'

'No,' he said, 'we won't write. I couldn't stand that. Some day I'll come back.'

'I'll never forget you, George.'

They reached the station, and she went with him while he bought his ticket. . . .

'Why, George O'Kelly and Jonquil Cary!'

It was a man and a girl whom George had known when he had worked in town, and Jonquil seemed to greet their presence with relief. For an interminable five minutes they all stood there talking; then the train roared into the station, and with ill-concealed agony in his face George held out his arms towards Jonquil. She took an uncertain step towards him, faltered, and then pressed his hand quickly as if she were taking leave of a chance friend.

'Good-bye, George,' she was saying, 'I hope you have a pleasant trip.

'Good-bye, George. Come back and see us all again.'

Dumb, almost blind with pain, he seized his suitcase, and in some dazed way got himself aboard the train.

Past clanging street-crossings, gathering speed through wide suburban spaces towards the sunset. Perhaps she too would see the sunset and pause for a moment, turning, remembering, before he faded with her sleep into the past. This night's dusk would cover up forever the sun and the trees and the flowers and laughter of his young world.

4

On a damp afternoon in September of the following year a young man with his face burned to a deep copper glow got off a train at a city in Tennessee. He looked around anxiously, and seemed relieved when he found that there was no one in the station to meet him. He taxied to the best hotel in the city where he registered with some satisfaction as George O'Kelly, Cuzco, Peru.

Up in his room he sat for a few minutes at the window looking down into the familiar street below. Then with his hand trembling faintly he took off the telephone receiver and called a number.

'Is Miss Jonquil in ?'

'This is she.'

'Oh –' His voice after overcoming a faint tendency to waver went on with friendly formality.

'This is George O'Kelly. Did you get my letter ?

'Yes. I thought you'd be in today.'

Her voice, cool and unmoved, disturbed him, but not as he had expected. This was the voice of a stranger, unexcited, pleasantly glad to see him – that was all. He wanted to put down the telephone and catch his breath.

'I haven't seen you for – a long time.' He succeeded in making this sound offhand. 'Over a year.'

He knew how long it had been – to the day.

'It'll be awfully nice to talk to you again.'

'I'll be there in about an hour.'

He hung up. For four long seasons every minute of his leisure had been crowded with anticipation of this hour, and now this hour was here. He had thought of finding her married, engaged, in love – he had not thought she would be unstirred at his return.

There would never again in his life, he felt, be another ten months like these he had just gone through. He had made an admittedly remarkable showing for a young engineer – stumbled into two unusual opportunities, one in Peru, whence he had just returned, and another consequent upon it, in New York, whither he was bound. In this short time he had risen from poverty into a position of unlimited opportunity.

He looked at himself in the dressing-table mirror. He was almost black with tan, but it was a romantic black, and in the last week, since he had had time to think it, it had given him considerable pleasure. The hardiness of his frame, too, he appraised with a sort of fascination. He had lost part of an eyebrow somewhere, and he still wore an elastic bandage on his knee, but he was too young not to realize that on the steamer many women had looked at him with unusual tributary interest.

His clothes, of course, were frightful. They had been made for him by a Greek tailor in Lima – in two days. He was young enough, too, to have explained this sartorial deficiency to Jonquil in his otherwise laconic note. The only further detail it contained was a request that he should *not* be met at the station.

George O'Kelly, of Cuzco, Peru, waited an hour and a half in the hotel, until, to be exact, the sun had reached a midway position in the sky. Then, freshly shaven and talcum-powdered towards a somewhat more Caucasian hue, for vanity at the last minute had overcome romance, he engaged a taxicab and set out for the house he knew so well.

He was breathing hard – he noticed this but he told himself that it was excitement, not emotion. He was here; she was not married – that was enough. He was not even sure what he had to say to her. But this was the moment of his life that he felt he could least easily have dispensed with. There was no triumph, after all, without a girl concerned, and if he did not lay his spoils at her feet he could at least hold them for a passing moment before her eyes.

The house loomed up suddenly beside him, and his first thought was that it had assumed a strange unreality. There was nothing changed – only everything was changed. It was smaller and it seemed shabbier than before – there was no cloud of magic hovering over its roof and issuing from the windows of the upper floor. He rang the doorbell and an unfamiliar coloured maid appeared. Miss Jonquil would be down in a moment. He wet his lips nervously and walked into the sitting-room – and the feeling of unreality increased. After all, he saw, this was only a room, and not the enchanted chamber where he had passed those poignant hours. He sat in a chair, amazed to find it a chair, realizing that his imagination had distorted and coloured all these simple familiar things.

Then the door opened and Jonquil came into the room – and it was as though everything in it suddenly blurred before his eyes. He had not remembered how beautiful she was, and he felt his face grow pale and his voice diminish to a poor sigh in his throat.

She was dressed in pale green, and a gold ribbon bound back her dark, straight hair like a crown. The familiar velvet eyes caught his as she came through the door, and a spasm of fright went through him at her beauty's power of inflicting pain.

He said 'Hello', and they each took a few steps forward and shook hands. Then they sat in chairs quite far apart and gazed at each other across the room.

'You've come back,' she said, and he answered just as tritely : 'I wanted to stop in and see you as I came through.'

He tried to neutralize the tremor in his voice by looking anywhere but at her face. The obligation to speak was on him, but, unless he immediately began to boast, it seemed that there was nothing to say. There had never been anything casual in their previous relations – it didn't seem possible that people in this position would talk about the weather.

'This is ridiculous,' he broke out in sudden embarrassment. 'I don't know exactly what to do. Does my being here bother you ?'

'No.' The answer was both reticent and impersonally sad. It depressed him.

'Are you engaged?' he demanded.

'No.'

'Are you in love with someone?'

She shook her head.

'Oh.' He leaned back in his chair. Another subject seemed exhausted – the interview was not taking the course he had intended.

'Jonquil,' he began, this time on a softer key, 'after all that's happened between us, I wanted to come back and see you. Whatever I do in the future I'll never love another girl as I've loved you.'

This was one of the speeches he had rehearsed. On the steamer it had seemed to have just the right note – a reference to the tenderness he would always feel for her combined with a non-committal attitude towards his present state of mind. Here with the past around him, beside him, growing minute by minute more heavy on the air, it seemed theatrical and stale.

She made no comment, sat without moving, her eyes fixed on him with an expression that might have meant everything or nothing.

'You don't love me any more, do you?' he asked her in a level voice.

'No.'

When Mrs Cary came in a minute later, and spoke to him about his success – there had been a half-column about him in the local paper – he was a mixture of emotions. He knew now that he still wanted this girl, and he knew that the past sometimes comes back – that was all. For the rest he must be strong and watchful and he would see.

'And now,' Mrs Cary was saying, 'I want you two to go and see the lady who has the chrysanthemums. She particularly told me she wanted to see you because she'd read about you in the paper.'

They went to see the lady with the chrysanthemums. They walked along the street, and he recognized with a sort of excitement just how her shorter footsteps always fell in between his own. The lady turned out to be nice, and the chrysanthemums were enormous and extraordinarily beautiful. The lady's gardens were full of them, white and pink and yellow, so that to be among them was a trip back into the heart of summer. There were two gardens full, and a gate between them; when they strolled towards the second garden the lady went first through the gate.

And then a curious thing happened. George stepped aside to let Jonquil pass, but instead of going through she stood still and stared at him for a minute. It was not so much the look, which was not a smile, as it was the moment of silence. They saw each other's eyes, and both took a short, faintly accelerated breath, and then they went on into the second garden. That was all.

The afternoon waned. They thanked the lady and walked home slowly, thoughtfully, side by side. Through dinner, too, they were silent. George told Mr Cary something of what had happened in South America, and managed to let it be known that everything would be plain sailing for him in the future.

Then dinner was over, and he and Jonquil were alone in the room which had seen the beginning of their love affair and the end. It seemed to him long ago and inexpressibly sad. On the sofa he had felt agony and grief such as he would never feel again. He would never be so weak or so tired and miserable and poor. Yet he knew that that boy of fifteen months before had had something, a trust, a warmth that was gone forever. The sensible thing – they had done the sensible thing. He had traded his youth for strength and carved success out of despair. But with his youth, life had carried away the freshness of his love.

'You won't marry me, will you?' he said quietly.

Jonquil shook her dark head.

'I'm never going to marry,' she answered.

He nodded.

'I'm going on to Washington in the morning,' he said.

'Oh –'

'I have to go. I've got to be in New York by the first, and meanwhile I want to stop off in Washington.'

'Business!'

'No-o,' he said as if reluctantly. 'There's someone there I must see who was very kind to me when I was so – down and out.'

This was invented. There was no one in Washington for him to see – but he was watching Jonquil narrowly, and he was sure that she winced a little, that her eyes closed and then opened wide again.

'But before I go I want to tell you the things that happened to me since I saw you, and, as maybe we won't meet again, I wonder if – if just this once you'd sit in my lap like you used to. I wouldn't ask except since there's no one else – yet – perhaps it doesn't matter.'

She nodded, and in a moment was sitting in his lap as she had sat so often in that vanished spring. The feel of her head against his shoulder, of her familiar body, sent a shock of emotion over him. His arms holding her had a tendency to tighten around her, so he leaned back and began to talk thoughtfully into the air.

He told her of a despairing two weeks in New York which had terminated with an attractive if not very profitable job in a construction plant in Jersey City. When the Peru business had first presented itself it had not seemed an extraordinary opportunity. He was to be third assistant engineer on the expedition, but only ten of the American party, including eight rodmen and surveyors, had ever reached Cuzco. Ten days later the chief of the expedition was dead of yellow fever. That had been his chance, a chance for anybody but a fool, a marvellous chance –

'A chance for anybody but a fool?' she interrupted innocently.

'Even for a fool,' he continued. 'It was wonderful. Well, I wired New York –'

'And so,' she interrupted again, 'they wired that you ought to take a chance?'

'Ought to!' he exclaimed, still leaning back. 'That I *had* to. There was no time to lose –'

'Not a minute?'

'Not a minute.'

'Not even time for –' she paused.

'For what?'

'Look.'

He bent his head forward suddenly, and she drew herself to him in the same moment, her lips half open like a flower.

'Yes,' he whispered into her lips. 'There's all the time in the world. . . .'

All the time in the world – his life and hers. But for an instant as he kissed her he knew that though he search through eternity he could never recapture those lost April hours. He might press her close now till the muscles knotted on his arms – she was something desirable and rare that he had fought for and made his own – but never again an intangible whisper in the dusk, or on the breeze of night. . . .

Well, let it pass, he thought; April is over, April is over. There are all kinds of love in the world, but never the same love twice.

Absolution

I

There was once a priest with cold, watery eyes, who, in the still of the night, wept cold tears. He wept because the afternoons were warm and long, and he was unable to attain a complete mystical union with our Lord. Sometimes, near four o'clock, there was a rustle of Swede girls along the path by his window, and in their shrill laughter he found a terrible dissonance that made him pray aloud for the twilight to come. At twilight the laughter and the voices were quieter, but several times he had walked past Romberg's Drug Store when it was dusk and the yellow lights shone inside and the nickel taps of the soda-fountain were gleaming, and he had found the scent of cheap toilet soap desperately sweet on the air. He passed that way when he returned from hearing confessions on Saturday nights, and he grew careful to walk on the other side of the street so that the smell of the soap would float upward before it reached his nostrils as it drifted, rather like incense, towards the summer moon.

But there was no escape from the hot madness of four o'clock. From his window, as far as he could see, the Dakota wheat thronged the valley of the Red River. The wheat was terrible to look upon and the carpet pattern to which in agony he bent his eyes sent his thought brooding through grotesque labyrinths, open always to the unavoidable sun.

One afternoon when he had reached the point where the mind runs down like an old clock, his housekeeper brought into his study a beautiful, intense little boy of eleven named Rudolph Miller. The little boy sat down in a patch of sunshine, and the priest, at his walnut desk, pretended to be very busy. This was to conceal his relief that some one had come into his haunted room.

Presently he turned around and found himself staring into two enormous, staccato eyes, lit with gleaming points of cobalt light. For a moment their expression startled him – then he saw that his visitor was in a state of abject fear.

'Your mouth is trembling,' said Father Schwartz, in a haggard voice.

The little boy covered his quivering mouth with his hand.

'Are you in trouble?' asked Father Schwartz, sharply. 'Take your hand away from your mouth and tell me what's the matter.'

The boy – Father Schwartz recognized him now as the son of a parishioner, Mr Miller, the freight-agent – moved his hand reluctantly off his mouth and became articulate in a despairing whisper.

'Father Schwartz – I've committed a terrible sin.'

'A sin against purity?'

'No, Father . . . worse.'

Father Schwartz's body jerked sharply.

'Have you killed somebody?'

'No – but I'm afraid –' the voice rose to a shrill whimper.

'Do you want to go to confession?'

The little boy shook his head miserably. Father Schwartz cleared his throat so that he could make his voice soft and say some quiet, kind thing. In this moment he should forget his own agony, and try to act like God. He repeated to himself a devotional phrase, hoping that in return God would help him to act correctly.

'Tell me what you've done,' said his new soft voice.

The little boy looked at him through his tears, and was reassured by the impression of moral resiliency which the distraught priest had created. Abandoning as much of himself as he was able to this man, Rudolph Miller began to tell his story.

'On Saturday, three days ago, my father he said I had to go to confession, because I hadn't been for a month, and the family they go every week, and I hadn't been. So I just as leave go, I didn't care. So I put it off till after supper because I was playing with a bunch of kids and father asked me if I went, and I said "no", and he took me by the neck and he said "You go now", so I said "All right", so I went over to church. And he yelled after me: "Don't come back till you go" ...'

2

'*On Saturday, Three Days Ago*'

The plush curtain of the confessional rearranged its dismal creases, leaving exposed only the bottom of an old man's shoe. Behind the curtain an immortal soul was alone with God and the Reverend Adolphus Schwartz, priest of the parish. Sound began, a laboured whispering, sibilant and discreet, broken at intervals by the voice of the priest in audible question.

Rudolph Miller knelt in the pew beside the confessional and waited, straining nervously to hear, and yet not to hear what was being said within. The fact that the priest was audible alarmed him. His own turn came next, and the three or four others who waited might listen unscrupulously while he admitted his violations of the Sixth and Ninth Commandments.

Rudolph had never committed adultery, nor even coveted his neighbour's wife – but it was the confession of the associate sins that was particularly hard to contemplate. In comparison he relished the less shameful fallings away – they formed a greyish background which relieved the ebony mark of sexual offences upon his soul.

He had been covering his ears with his hands, hoping that his refusal to hear would be noticed, and a like courtesy rendered to him in turn, when a sharp movement of the penitent in the confessional made him sink his face precipitately into the crook of his elbow. Fear assumed solid form, and pressed out a lodging between his heart and his lungs. He must try now with all his might to be sorry for his sins – not because he was afraid, but because he had offended God. He must convince God that he was sorry and to do so he must first convince himself. After a tense emotional struggle he achieved a tremulous self-pity, and decided that he was now ready. If, by allowing no other thought to enter his head, he could preserve this state of emotion unimpaired until he went into that large coffin set on end, he would have survived another crisis in his religious life.

For some time, however, a demoniac notion had partially possessed him. He could go home now, before his turn came, and tell his mother that he had arrived too late, and found the priest gone. This, unfortunately, involved the risk of being caught in a lie. As an alternative he could say that he *had* gone to confession, but this meant that he must avoid communion next day, for communion taken upon an uncleansed soul would turn to poison in his mouth, and he would crumple limp and damned from the altar-rail.

Again Father Schwartz's voice became audible.

'And for your –'

The words blurred to a husky mumble, and Rudolph got excitedly to his feet. He felt that it was impossible to go to confession this afternoon. He hesitated tensely. Then from the confessional came a tap, a creak, and a sustained rustle. The slide had fallen and the plush curtain trembled. Temptation had come to him too late. . . .

'Bless me, Father, for I have sinned. . . . I confess to Almighty God and to you, Father, that I have sinned. . . . Since my last confession it has been one month and three days. . . . I accuse myself of – taking the Name of the Lord in vain. . . .'

This was an easy sin. His curses had been but bravado – telling of them was little less than a brag.

'. . . of being mean to an old lady.'

The wan shadow moved a little on the latticed slat.

'How, my child ?'

'Old Lady Swenson,' Rudolph's murmur soared jubilantly. 'She got our baseball that we knocked in her window, and she wouldn't give it back, so we yelled "Twenty-three, Skidoo," at her all afternoon. Then about five o'clock she had a fit, and they had to have the doctor.'

'Go on, my child.'

'Of – of not believing I was the son of my parents.'

'What ?' The interrogation was distinctly startled.

'Of not believing that I was the son of my parents.'

'Why not?'

'Oh, just pride,' answered the penitent airily.

'You mean you thought yourself too good to be the son of your parents?'

'Yes, Father.' On a less jubilant note.

'Go on.'

'Of being disobedient and calling my mother names. Of slandering people behind their back. Of smoking –'

Rudolph had now exhausted the minor offences, and was approaching the sins it was agony to tell. He held his fingers against his face like bars as if to press out between them the shame in his heart.

'Of dirty words and immodest thoughts and desires,' he whispered very low .

'How often?'

'I don't know.'

'Once a week? Twice a week?'

'Twice a week.'

'Did you yield to these desires?'

'No, Father.'

'Were you alone when you had them?'

'No, Father. I was with two boys and a girl.'

'Don't you know, my child, that you should avoid the occasions of sin as well as the sin itself? Evil companionship leads to evil desires and evil desires to evil actions. Where were you when this happened?'

'In a barn back of –'

'I don't want to hear any names,' interrupted the priest sharply.

'Well, it was up in the loft of this barn and this girl and – a fella, they were saying things – saying immodest things, and I stayed.'

'You should have gone – you should have told the girl to go.'

He should have gone! He could not tell Father Schwartz how his pulse had bumped in his wrist, how a strange, romantic excitement had possessed him when those curious things had been said. Perhaps, in the houses of delinquency, among the dull and hard-eyed incorrigible girls can be found those for whom has burned the whitest fire.

'Have you anything else to tell me?'

'I don't think so, Father.'

Rudolph felt a great relief. Perspiration had broken out under his tight-pressed fingers.

'Have you told any lies?'

The question startled him. Like all those who habitually and instinctively lie, he had an enormous respect and awe for the truth. Something almost exterior to himself dictated a quick, hurt answer. 'Oh no, Father, I never tell lies.'

For a moment, like the commoner in the king's chair, he tasted the pride of the situation. Then as the priest began to murmur conventional admonitions he realized that in heroically denying he had told lies, he had committed a terrible sin – he had told a lie in confession.

In automatic response to Father Schwartz's 'Make an act of contrition', he began to repeat aloud meaninglessly:

'Oh, my God, I am heartily sorry for having offended Thee. . . .'

He must fix this now – it was a bad mistake – but as his teeth shut on the last words of his prayer there was a sharp sound, and the slat was closed.

A minute later when he emerged into the twilight the relief in coming from the muggy church into an open world of wheat and sky postponed the full realization of what he had done. Instead of worrying he took a deep breath of the crisp air and began to say over and over to himself the words 'Blatchford Sarnemington, Blatchford Sarnemington!'

Blatchford Sarnemington was himself, and these words were in effect a lyric. When he became Blatchford Sarnemington a sauve nobility flowed from him. Blatchford Sarnemington lived in great sweeping triumphs. When Rudolph half closed his eyes it meant that Blatchford had established dominance over him and, as he went by, there were envious mutters in the air:

'Blatchford Sarnemington! There goes Blatchford Sarnemington.'

He was Blatchford now for a while as he strutted homeward along the staggering road, but when the road braced itself in macadam in order to become the main street of Ludwig, Rudolph's exhilaration faded out and his mind cooled, and he felt the horror of his lie. God, of course, already knew of it – but Rudolph reserved a corner of his mind where he was safe from God, where he prepared the subterfuges with which he often tricked God. Hiding now in this corner he considered how he could best avoid the consequences of his mis-statement.

At all costs he must avoid communion next day. The risk of angering God to such an extent was too great. He would have to drink water 'by accident' in the morning, and thus, in accordance with a church law, render himself unfit to receive communion that day. In spite of its flimsiness this subterfuge was the most feasible that occurred to him. He accepted its risks and was concentrating on how best to put it into effect, as he turned the corner by Romberg's Drug Store and came in sight of his father's house.

3

Rudolph's father, the local freight-agent, had floated with the second wave of German and Irish stock to the Minnesota–Dakota country. Theoretically, great opportunities lay ahead of a young man of energy in that day and place, but Carl Miller had been incapable of establishing either with his superiors or his subordinates the reputation for approximate immutability which is essential to success in a hierarchic industry. Somewhat gross, he was, nevertheless, insufficiently hard-headed and unable to take fundamental relationships for granted, and this inability made him suspicious, unrestful, and continually dismayed.

His two bonds with the colourful life were his faith in the Roman Catholic Church and his mystical worship of the Empire Builder, James J. Hill. Hill was the apotheosis of that quality in which Miller himself was deficient – the sense of things, the feel of things, the hint of rain in the wind on the cheek. Miller's mind worked late on the old decisions of other men, and he had never in his life felt the balance of any single thing in his hands. His weary, sprightly, undersized body was growing old in Hill's gigantic shadow. For twenty years he had lived alone with Hill's name and God.

On Sunday morning Carl Miller awoke in the dustless quiet of six o'clock. Kneeling by the side of the bed he bent his yellow-grey hair and the full dapple bangs of his moustache into the pillow, and prayed for several minutes. Then he drew off his night-shirt – like the rest of his generation he had never been able to endure pyjamas – and clothed his thin, white, hairless body in woollen underwear.

He shaved. Silence in the other bedroom where his wife lay nervously asleep. Silence from the screened-off corner of the hall where his son's cot stood, and his son slept among his Alger books, his collection of cigar-bands, his mothy pennants – 'Cornell', 'Hamlin', and 'Greetings from Pueblo, New Mexico' – and the other possessions of his private life. From outside Miller could hear the shrill birds and the whirring movement of the poultry, and, as an undertone, the low, swelling click-a-click of the six-fifteen through train for Montana and the green coast beyond. Then as the cold water dripped from the wash-rag in his hand he raised his head suddenly – he had heard a furtive sound from the kitchen below.

He dried his razor hastily, slipped his dangling suspenders to his shoulder, and listened. Some one was walking in the kitchen, and he knew by the light footfall that it was not his wife. With his mouth faintly ajar he ran quickly down the stairs and opened the kitchen door.

Standing by the sink, with one hand on the still dripping faucet and the other clutching a full glass of water, stood his son. The boy's eyes, still heavy with sleep, met his father's with a frightened, reproachful beauty. He was barefooted, and his pyjamas were rolled up at the knees and sleeves.

For a moment they both remained motionless – Carl Miller's

brow went down and his son's went up, as though they were striking a balance between the extremes of emotion which filled them. Then the bangs of the parent's moustache descended portentously until they obscured his mouth, and he gave a short glance around to see if anything had been disturbed.

The kitchen was garnished with sunlight which beat on the pans and made the smooth boards of the floor and table yellow and clean as wheat. It was the centre of the house where the fire burned and the tins fitted into tins like toys, and the steam whistled all day on a thin pastel note. Nothing was moved, nothing touched – except the faucet where beads of water still formed and dripped with a white flash into the sink below.

'What are you doing?'

'I got awful thirsty, so I thought I'd just come down and get –'

'I thought you were going to communion.'

A look of vehement astonishment spread over his son's face.

'I forgot all about it.'

'Have you drunk any water?'

'No –'

As the word left his mouth Rudolph knew it was the wrong answer, but the faded indignant eyes facing him had signalled up the truth before the boy's will could act. He realized, too, that he should never have come downstairs; some vague necessity for verisimilitude had made him want to leave a wet glass as evidence by the sink; the honesty of his imagination had betrayed him.

'Pour it out,' commanded his father, 'that water!'

Rudolph despairingly inverted the tumbler.

'What's the matter with you, anyways?' demanded Miller angrily.

'Nothing.'

'Did you go to confession yesterday?'

'Yes.'

'Then why were you going to drink water?'

'I don't know – I forgot.'

'Maybe you care more about being a little thirsty than you do about your religion.'

'I forgot.' Rudolph could feel the tears straining in his eyes.

'That's no answer.'

'Well, I did.'

'You better look out!' His father held to a high, persistent inquisitory note: 'If you're so forgetful that you can't remember your religion something better be done about it.'

Rudolph filled a sharp pause with:

'I can remember it all right.'

'First you begin to neglect your religion,' cried his father, fanning his own fierceness, 'the next thing you'll begin to lie and steal, and the *next* thing is the *reform* school!'

Not even this familiar threat could deepen the abyss that Rudolph saw before him. He must either tell all now, offering his body for what he knew would be a ferocious beating or else tempt the thunderbolts by receiving the Body and Blood of Christ with sacrilege upon his soul. And of the two the former seemed more terrible – it was not so much the beating he dreaded as the savage ferocity, outlet of the ineffectual man, which would lie behind it.

'Put down that glass and go upstairs and dress!' his father ordered, 'and when we get to church, before you go to communion, you better kneel down and ask God to forgive you for your carelessness.'

Some accidental emphasis in the phrasing of this command acted like a catalytic agent on the confusion and terror of Rudolph's mind. A wild, proud anger rose in him, and he dashed the tumbler passionately into the sink.

His father uttered a strained, husky sound, and sprang for him. Rudolph dodged to the side, tipped over a chair, and tried to get beyond the kitchen table. He cried out sharply when a hand grasped his pyjama shoulder, then he felt the dull impact of a fist against the side of his head, and glancing blows on the upper part of his body. As he slipped here and there in his father's grasp, dragged or lifted when he clung instinctively to an arm, aware of sharp smarts and strains, he made no sound except that he laughed hysterically several times. Then in less than a minute the blows abruptly ceased. After a lull during which Rudolph was tightly held, and during which they both trembled violently and uttered strange, truncated words, Carl Miller half dragged, half threatened his son upstairs.

'Put on your clothes!'

Rudolph was now both hysterical and cold. His head hurt him, and there was a long, shallow scratch on his neck from his father's fingernail, and he sobbed and trembled as he dressed. He was aware of his mother standing at the doorway in a wrapper, her wrinkled face compressing and squeezing and opening out into new series of wrinkles which floated and eddied from neck to brow. Despising her nervous ineffectuality and avoiding her rudely when she tried to touch his cheek with witch-hazel, he made a hasty, choking toilet. Then he followed his father out of the house and along the road towards the Catholic church.

4

They walked without speaking except when Carl Miller acknowledged automatically the existence of passers-by. Rudolph's uneven breathing alone ruffled the hot Sunday silence.

His father stopped decisively at the door of the church.

'I've decided you'd better go to confession again. Go and tell Father Schwartz what you did and ask God's pardon.'

'You lost your temper, too!' said Rudolph quickly.

Carl Miller took a step towards his son, who moved cautiously backward.

'All right, I'll go.'

'Are you going to do what I say?' cried his father in a hoarse whisper.

'All right.'

Rudolph walked into the church, and for the second time in two days entered the confessional and knelt down. The slat went up almost at once.

'I accuse myself of missing my morning prayers.'

'Is that all?'

'That's all.'

A maudlin exultation filled him. Not easily ever again would he be able to put an abstraction before the necessities of his ease and pride. An invisible line had been crossed, and he had become aware of his isolation – aware that it applied not only to those moments when he was Blatchford Sarnemington but that it applied to all his inner life. Hitherto such phenomena as 'crazy' ambitions and petty shames and fears had been but private reservations, unacknowledged before the throne of his official soul. Now he realized unconsciously that his private reservations were himself – and all the rest a garnished front and a conventional flag. The pressure of his environment had driven him into the lonely secret road of adolescence.

He knelt in the pew beside his father. Mass began. Rudolph knelt up – when he was alone he slumped his posterior back against the seat – and tasted the consciousness of a sharp, subtle revenge. Beside him his father prayed that God would forgive Rudolph, and asked also that his own outbreak of temper would be pardoned. He glanced sidewise at his son, and was relieved to see that the strained, wild look had gone from his face and that he had ceased sobbing. The Grace of God, inherent in the Sacrament, would do the rest, and perhaps after Mass everything would be better. He was proud of Rudolph in his heart, and beginning to be truly as well as formally sorry for what he had done.

Usually, the passing of the collection box was the significant point for Rudolph in the services. If, as was often the case, he had no money to drop in he would be furiously ashamed and bow his head and pretend not to see the box, lest Jeanne Brady in the pew behind should take notice and suspect an acute family poverty. But today he glanced coldly into it as it skimmed under his eyes, noting with casual interest the large number of pennies it contained.

When the bell rang for communion, however, he quivered. There was no reason why God should not stop his heart.

During the past twelve hours he had committed a series of mortal sins increasing in gravity, and he was now to crown them all with a blasphemous sacrilege.

'*Domine, non sum dignus; ut intres sub tectum meum; sed tantum dic verbo, et sanabitur anima mea. . . .*'

There was a rustle in the pews, and the communicants worked their ways into the aisle with downcast eyes and joined hands. Those of larger piety pressed together their finger-tips to form steeples. Among these latter was Carl Miller. Rudolph followed him towards the altar-rail and knelt down, automatically taking up the napkin under his chin. The bell rang sharply, and the priest turned from the altar with the white Host held above the chalice :

'*Corpus Domini nostri Jesu Christi custodiat animam tuam in vitam aeternam.*'

A cold sweat broke out on Rudolph's forehead as the communion began. Along the line Father Schwartz moved, and with gathering nausea Rudolph felt his heart-valves weakening at the will of God. It seemed to him that the church was darker and that a great quiet had fallen, broken only by the inarticulate mumble which announced the approach of the Creator of Heaven and Earth. He dropped his head down between his shoulders and waited for the blow.

Then he felt a sharp nudge in his side. His father was poking him to sit up, not to slump against the rail; the priest was only two places away.

'*Corpus Domini nostri Jesu Christi custodiat animam tuam in vitam aeternam.*'

Rudolph opened his mouth. He felt the sticky wax taste of the wafer on his tongue. He remained motionless for what seemed an interminable period of time, his head still raised, the wafer undissolved in his mouth. Then again he started at the pressure of his father's elbow, and saw that the people were falling away from the altar like leaves and turning with blind downcast eyes to their pews, alone with God.

Rudolph was alone with himself, drenched with perspiration and deep in mortal sin. As he walked back to his pew the sharp taps of his cloven hoofs were loud upon the floor, and he knew that it was a dark poison he carried in his heart.

5

'Sagitta Volante in Dei'

The beautiful little boy with eyes like blue stones, and lashes that sprayed open from them like flower-petals, had finished telling his sin to Father Schwartz – and the square of sunshine in which he sat had moved forward an hour into the room. Rudolph had become less frightened now; once eased of the story a reaction had set in. He knew that as long as he was in the room with this priest God would not stop his heart, so he sighed and sat quietly, waiting for the priest to speak.

Father Schwartz's cold watery eyes were fixed upon the carpet pattern on which the sun had brought out the swastikas and the flat bloomless vines and the pale echoes of flowers. The hall-clock ticked insistently towards sunset, and from the ugly room and from the afternoon outside the window arose a stiff monotony, shattered now and then by the reverberate clapping of a far-away hammer on the dry air. The priest's nerves were strung thin and the beads of his rosary were crawling and squirming like snakes upon the green felt of his table top. He could not remember now what it was he should say.

Of all the things in this lost Swede town he was most aware of this little boy's eyes – the beautiful eyes, with lashes that left them reluctantly and curved back as though to meet them once more.

For a moment longer the silence persisted while Rudolph waited, and the priest struggled to remember something that was slipping farther and farther away from him, and the clock ticked in the broken house. Then Father Schwartz stared hard at the little boy and remarked in a peculiar voice:

'When a lot of people get together in the best places things go glimmering.'

Rudolph started and looked quickly at Father Schwartz's face.

'I said –' began the priest, and paused, listening. 'Do you

hear the hammer and the clock ticking and the bees? Well, that's no good. The thing is to have a lot of people in the centre of the world, wherever that happens to be. Then' – his watery eyes widened knowingly – 'things go glimmering.'

'Yes, Father,' agreed Rudolph, feeling a little frightened.

'What are you going to be when you grow up?'

'Well, I was going to be a baseball-player for a while,' answered Rudolph nervously, 'but I don't think that is a very good ambition, so I think I'll be an actor or a Navy officer.'

Again the priest stared at him.

'I see *exactly* what you mean,' he said, with a fierce air.

Rudolph had not meant anything in particular, and at the implication that he had, he became more uneasy.

'This man is crazy,' he thought, 'and I'm scared of him. He wants me to help him out some way, and I don't want to.'

'You look as if things went glimmering,' cried Father Schwartz wildly. 'Did you ever go to a party?'

'Yes, Father.'

'And did you notice that everybody was properly dressed? That's what I mean. Just as you went into the party there was a moment when everybody was properly dressed. Maybe two little girls were standing by the door and some boys were leaning over the banisters, and there were bowls around full of flowers.'

'I've been to a lot of parties,' said Rudolph, rather relieved that the conversation had taken this turn.

'Of course,' continued Father Schwartz triumphantly, 'I knew you'd agree with me. But my theory is that when a whole lot of people get together in the best places things go glimmering all the time.'

Rudolph found himself thinking of Blatchford Sarnemington.

'Please listen to me!' commanded the priest impatiently. 'Stop worrying about last Saturday. Apostasy implies an absolute damnation only on the supposition of a previous perfect faith. Does that fix it?'

Rudolph had not the faintest idea what Father Schwartz

was talking about, but he nodded and the priest nodded back at him and returned to his mysterious preoccupation.

'Why,' he cried, 'they have lights now as big as stars – do you realize that? I heard of one light they had in Paris or somewhere that was as big as a star. A lot of people had it – a lot of gay people. They have all sorts of things now that you never dreamed of.'

'Look here –' He came nearer to Rudolph, but the boy drew away, so Father Schwartz went back and sat down in his chair, his eyes dried out and hot. 'Did you ever see an amusement park?'

'No, Father.'

'Well, go and see an amusement park.' The priest waved his hand vaguely. 'It's a thing like a fair, only much more glittering. Go to one at night and stand a little way off from it in a dark place – under dark trees. You'll see a big wheel made of lights turning in the air, and a long slide shooting boats down into the water. A band playing somewhere, and a smell of peanuts – and everything will twinkle. But it won't remind you of anything, you see. It will all just hang out there in the night like a coloured balloon – like a big yellow lantern on a pole.'

Father Schwartz frowned as he suddenly thought of something.

'But don't get up close,' he warned Rudolph, 'because if you do you'll only feel the heat and the sweat and the life.'

All this talking seemed particularly strange and awful to Rudolph, because this man was a priest. He sat there, half terrified, his beautiful eyes open wide and staring at Father Schwartz. But underneath his terror he felt that his own inner convictions were confirmed. There was something ineffably gorgeous somewhere that had nothing to do with God. He no longer thought that God was angry at him about the original lie, because He must have understood that Rudolph had done it to make things finer in the confessional, brightening up the dinginess of his admissions by saying a thing radiant and proud. At the moment when he had affirmed immaculate honour a silver pennon had flapped out into the breeze somewhere and there had been the crunch of leather and the shine of silver spurs and a troop of horsemen waiting for dawn on a low green hill. The sun had made stars of light on their breastplates like the picture at home of the German cuirassiers at Sedan.

But now the priest was muttering inarticulate and heartbroken words, and the boy became wildly afraid. Horror entered suddenly in at the open window, and the atmosphere of the room changed. Father Schwartz collapsed precipitously down on his knees, and let his body settle back against a chair.

'Oh, my God!' he cried out, in a strange voice, and wilted to the floor.

Then a human oppression rose from the priest's worn clothes, and mingled with the faint smell of old food in the corners. Rudolph gave a sharp cry and ran in panic from the house – while the collapsed man lay there quite still, filling his room, filling it with voices and faces until it was crowded with echolalia, and rang loud with a steady shrill note of laughter.

Outside the window the blue sirocco trembled over the wheat, and girls with yellow hair walked sensuously along roads that bounded the fields, calling innocent, exciting things to the young men who were working in the lines between the grain. Legs were shaped under starchless gingham, and rims of the necks of dresses were warm and damp. For five hours now hot fertile life had burned in the afternoon. It would be night in three hours, and all along the land there would be those blonde Northern girls and the tall young men from the farms lying out beside the wheat, under the moon.

The Baby Party

When John Andros felt old he found solace in the thought of
life continuing through his child. The dark trumpets of oblivion
were less loud at the patter of his child's feet or at the sound of
his child's voice babbling mad non sequiturs to him over the
telephone. The latter incident occurred every afternoon at three
when his wife called the office from the country, and he came
to look forward to it as one of the vivid minutes of his day.

He was not physically old, but his life had been a series of
struggles up a series of rugged hills, and here at thirty-eight
having won his battles against ill-health and poverty he
cherished less than the usual number of illusions. Even his feeling about his little girl was qualified. She had interrupted his
rather intense love-affair with his wife, and she was the reason
for their living in a suburban town, where they paid for country
air with endless servant troubles and the weary merry-go-round
of the commuting train.

It was little Ede as a definite piece of youth that chiefly interested him. He liked to take her on his lap and examine minutely
her fragrant, downy scalp and her eyes with their irises of
morning blue. Having paid this homage John was content that
the nurse should take her away. After ten minutes the very
vitality of the child irritated him; he was inclined to lose his
temper when things were broken, and one Sunday afternoon
when she had disrupted a bridge game by permanently hiding
up the ace of spades, he had made a scene that had reduced
his wife to tears.

This was absurd and John was ashamed of himself. It was
inevitable that such things would happen, and it was impossible
that little Ede should spend all her indoor hours in the nursery

upstairs when she was becoming, as her mother said, more nearly a 'real person' every day.

She was two and a half, and this afternoon, for instance, she was going to a baby party. Grown-up Edith, her mother, had telephoned the information to the office, and little Ede had confirmed the business by shouting 'I yam going to a *pantry*!' into John's unsuspecting left ear.

'Drop in at the Markeys' when you get home, won't you, dear?' resumed her mother. 'It'll be funny. Ede's going to be all dressed up in her new pink dress –'

The conversation terminated abruptly with a squawk which indicated that the telephone had been pulled violently to the floor. John laughed and decided to get an early train out; the prospect of a baby party in someone else's house amused him.

'What a peach of a mess!' he thought humorously. 'A dozen mothers, and each one looking at nothing but her own child. All the babies breaking things and grabbing at the cake, and each mama going home thinking about the subtle superiority of her own child to every other child there.'

He was in a good humour today – all the things in his life were going better than they had ever gone before. When he got off the train at his station he shook his head at an importunate taxi man, and began to walk up the long hill towards his house through the crisp December twilight. It was only six o'clock but the moon was out, shining with proud brilliance on the thin sugary snow that lay over the lawns.

As he walked along drawing his lungs full of cold air his happiness increased, and the idea of a baby party appealed to him more and more. He began to wonder how Ede compared to other children of her own age, and if the pink dress she was to wear was something radical and mature. Increasing his gait he came in sight of his own house, where the lights of a defunct Christmas-tree still blossomed in the window, but he continued on past the walk. The party was at the Markeys' next door.

As he mounted the brick step and rang the bell he became aware of voices inside, and he was glad he was not too late.

Then he raised his head and listened – the voices were not children's voices, but they were loud and pitched high with anger; there were at least three of them and one, which rose as he listened to a hysterical sob, he recognized immediately as his wife's.

'There's been some trouble,' he thought quickly.

Trying the door, he found it unlocked and pushed it open.

The baby party started at half past four, but Edith Andros, calculating shrewdly that the new dress would stand out more sensationally against vestments already rumpled, planned the arrival of herself and little Ede for five. When they appeared it was already a flourishing affair. Four baby girls and nine baby boys, each one curled and washed and dressed with all the care of a proud and jealous heart, were dancing to the music of a phonograph. Never more than two or three were dancing at once, but as all were continually in motion running to and from their mothers for encouragement, the general effect was the same.

As Edith and her daughter entered, the music was temporarily drowned out by a sustained chorus, consisting largely of the word *cute* and directed towards little Ede, who stood looking timidly about and fingering the edges of her pink dress. She was not kissed – this is the sanitary age – but she was passed along a row of mamas each one of whom said 'cu-u-ute' to her and held her pink little hand before passing her on to the next. After some encouragement and a few mild pushes she was absorbed into the dance, and became an active member of the party.

Edith stood near the door talking to Mrs Markey, and keeping an eye on the tiny figure in the pink dress. She did not care for Mrs Markey; she considered her both snippy and common, but John and Joe Markey were congenial and went in together on the commuting train every morning, so the two women kept up an elaborate pretence of warm amity. They were always reproaching each other for 'not coming to see me', and they were always planning the kind of parties that began with

'You'll have to come to dinner with us soon, and we'll go to the theatre,' but never matured further.

'Little Ede looks perfectly darling,' said Mrs Markey, smiling and moistening her lips in a way that Edith found particularly repulsive. 'So *grown-up* – I can't *believe* it!'

Edith wondered if 'little Ede' referred to the fact that Billy Markey, though several months younger, weighed almost five pounds more. Accepting a cup of tea she took a seat with two other ladies on a divan and launched into the real business of the afternoon, which of course lay in relating the recent accomplishments and insouciances of her child.

An hour passed. Dancing palled and the babies took to sterner sport. They ran into the dining-room, rounded the big table, and essayed the kitchen door, from which they were rescued by an expeditionary force of mothers. Having been rounded up they immediately broke loose, and rushing back to the dining-room tried the familiar swinging door again. The word 'overheated' began to be used, and small white brows were dried with small white handkerchiefs. A general attempt to make the babies sit down began, but the babies squirmed off laps with peremptory cries of 'Down! Down!' and the rush into the fascinating dining-room began anew.

This phase of the party came to an end with the arrival of refreshments, a large cake with two candles, and saucers of vanilla ice-cream. Billy Markey, a stout laughing baby with red hair and legs somewhat bowed, blew out the candles, and placed an experimental thumb on the white frosting. The refreshments were distributed, and the children ate, greedily but without confusion – they had behaved remarkably well all afternoon. They were modern babies who ate and slept at regular hours, so their dispositions were good, and their faces healthy and pink – such a peaceful party would not have been possible thirty years ago.

After the refreshments a gradual exodus began. Edith glanced anxiously at her watch – it was almost six, and John had not arrived. She wanted him to see Ede with the other children – to see how dignified and polite and intelligent she was, and how the only ice-cream spot on her dress was some that had dropped from her chin when she was joggled from behind.

'You're a darling,' she whispered to her child, drawing her suddenly against her knee. 'Do you know you're a darling? Do you *know* you're a darling?'

Ede laughed. 'Bow-wow,' she said suddenly.

'Bow-wow?' Edith looked around. 'There isn't any bow-wow.'

'Bow-wow,' repeated Ede. 'I want a bow-wow.'

Edith followed the small pointing finger.

'That isn't a bow-wow, dearest, that's a teddy-bear.'

'Bear?'

'Yes, that's a teddy-bear, and it belongs to Billy Markey. You don't want Billy Markey's teddy-bear, do you?'

Ede did want it.

She broke away from her mother and approached Billy Markey, who held the toy closely in his arms. Ede stood regarding him with inscrutable eyes, and Billy laughed.

Grown-up Edith looked at her watch again, this time impatiently.

The party had dwindled until, besides Ede and Billy, there were only two babies remaining – and one of the two remained only by virtue of having hidden himself under the dining-room table. It was selfish of John not to come. It showed so little pride in the child. Other fathers had come, half a dozen of them, to call for their wives, and they had stayed for a while and looked on.

There was a sudden wail. Ede had obtained Billy's teddy-bear by pulling it forcibly from his arms, and on Billy's attempt to recover it, she had pushed him casually to the floor.

'Why, Ede!' cried her mother, repressing an inclination to laugh.

Joe Markey, a handsome, broad-shouldered man of thirty-five, picked up his son and set him on his feet. 'You're a fine fellow,' he said jovially. 'Let a girl knock you over! You're a fine fellow.'

'Did he bump his head?' Mrs Markey returned anxiously

from bowing the next to last remaining mother out of the door.

'No-o-o-o,' exclaimed Markey. 'He bumped something else, didn't you, Billy ? He bumped something else.'

Billy had so far forgotten the bump that he was already making an attempt to recover his property. He seized a leg of the bear which projected from Ede's enveloping arms and tugged at it but without success.

'No,' said Ede emphatically.

Suddenly, encouraged by the success of her former half-accidental manoeuvre, Ede dropped the teddy-bear, placed her hands on Billy's shoulders and pushed him backward off his feet.

This time he landed less harmlessly; his head hit the bare floor just off the rug with a dull hollow sound, whereupon he drew in his breath and delivered an agonized yell.

Immediately the room was in confusion. With an exclamation Markey hurried to his son, but his wife was first to reach the injured baby and catch him up into her arms.

'Oh, *Billy*,' she cried, 'what a terrible bump! She ought to be spanked.'

Edith, who had rushed immediately to her daughter, heard this remark, and her lips came sharply together.

'Why, Ede,' she whispered perfunctorily, 'you bad girl !'

Ede put back her little head suddenly and laughed. It was a loud laugh, a triumphant laugh with victory in it and challenge and contempt. Unfortunately it was also an infectious laugh. Before her mother realized the delicacy of the situation, she too had laughed, an audible, distinct laugh not unlike the baby's, and partaking of the same overtones.

Then, as suddenly, she stopped.

Mrs Markey's face had grown red with anger, and Markey, who had been feeling the back of the baby's head with one finger, looked at her, frowning.

'It's swollen already,' he said with a note of reproof in his voice. 'I'll get some witch-hazel.'

But Mrs Markey had lost her temper. 'I don't see anything funny about a child being hurt!' she said in a trembling voice.

Little Ede meanwhile had been looking at her mother curiously. She noted that her own laugh had produced her mother's and she wondered if the same cause would always produce the same effect. So she chose this moment to throw back her head and laugh again.

To her mother the additional mirth added the final touch of hysteria to the situation. Pressing her handkerchief to her mouth she giggled irrepressibly. It was more than nervousness – she felt that in a peculiar way she was laughing with her child – they were laughing together.

It was in a way a defiance – those two against the world.

While Markey rushed upstairs to the bathroom for ointment, his wife was walking up and down rocking the yelling boy in her arms.

'Please go home!' she broke out suddenly. 'The child's badly hurt, and if you haven't the decency to be quiet, you'd better go home.'

'Very well,' said Edith, her own temper rising. 'I've never seen anyone make such a mountain out of –'

'Get out!' cried Mrs Markey frantically. 'There's the door, get out – I never want to see you in our house again. You or your brat either!'

Edith had taken her daughter's hand and was moving quickly towards the door, but at this remark she stopped and turned around, her face contracting with indignation.

'Don't you dare call her that!'

Mrs Markey did not answer but continued walking up and down, muttering to herself and to Billy in an inaudible voice.

Edith began to cry.

'I will get out!' she sobbed, 'I've never heard anybody so rude and c-common in my life. I'm glad your baby did get pushed down – he's nothing but a f-fat little fool anyhow.'

Joe Markey reached the foot of the stairs just in time to hear this remark.

'Why, Mrs Andros,' he said sharply, 'can't you see the child's hurt. You really ought to control yourself.'

'Control m-myself!' exclaimed Edith brokenly. 'You better ask her to c-control herself. I've never heard anybody so c-common in my life.'

'She's insulting me!' Mrs Markey was now livid with rage. 'Did you hear what she said, Joe? I wish you'd put her out. If she won't go, just take her by the shoulders and put her out!'

'Don't you dare touch me!' cried Edith. 'I'm going just as quick as I can find my c-coat!'

Blind with tears she took a step towards the hall. It was just at this moment that the door opened and John Andros walked anxiously in.

'John!' cried Edith, and fled to him wildly.

'What's the matter? Why, what's the matter?'

'They're – they're putting me out!' she wailed, collapsing against him. 'He'd just started to take me by the shoulders and put me out. I want my coat!'

'That's not true,' objected Markey hurriedly. 'Nobody's going to put you out.' He turned to John. 'Nobody's going to put her out,' he repeated. 'She's –'

'What do you mean "put her out"?' demanded John abruptly. 'What's all this talk, anyhow?'

'Oh, let's go!' cried Edith. 'I want to go. They're so *common*, John!'

'Look here!' Markey's face darkened. 'You've said that about enough. You're acting sort of crazy.'

'They called Ede a brat!'

For the second time that afternoon little Ede expressed emotion at an inopportune moment. Confused and frightened at the shouting voices, she began to cry, and her tears had the effect of conveying that she felt the insult in her heart.

'What's the idea of this?' broke out John. 'Do you insult your guests in your own house?'

'It seems to me it's your wife that's done the insulting!' answered Markey crisply. 'In fact, your baby there started all the trouble.'

John gave a contemptuous snort. 'Are you calling names at a little baby?' he inquired. 'That's a fine manly business!'

'Don't talk to him, John,' insisted Edith. 'Find my coat!'

'You must be in a bad way,' went on John angrily, 'if you have to take out your temper on a helpless little baby.'

'I never heard anything so damn twisted in my life,' shouted Markey. 'If that wife of yours would shut her mouth for a minute –'

'Wait a minute! You're not talking to a woman and child now –'

There was an incidental interruption. Edith had been fumbling on a chair for her coat, and Mrs Markey had been watching her with hot, angry eyes. Suddenly she laid Billy down on the sofa, where he immediately stopped crying and pulled himself upright, and coming into the hall she quickly found Edith's coat and handed it to her without a word. Then she went back to the sofa, picked up Billy, and rocking him in her arms looked again at Edith with hot, angry eyes. The interruption had taken less than half a minute.

'Your wife comes in here and begins shouting around about how common we are!' burst out Markey violently. 'Well, if we're so damn common, you'd better stay away! And what's more, you'd better get out now!'

Again John gave a short, contemptuous laugh.

'You're not only common,' he returned, 'you're evidently an awful bully – when there's any helpless women and children around.' He felt for the knob and swung the door open. 'Come on, Edith.'

Taking up her daughter in her arms, his wife stepped outside and John, still looking contemptuously at Markey, started to follow.

'Wait a minute!' Markey took a step forward; he was trembling slightly, and two large veins on his temples were suddenly full of blood. 'You don't think you can get away with that, do you? With me?'

Without a word John walked out the door, leaving it open.

Edith, still weeping, had started for home. After following

her with his eyes until she reached her own walk, John turned back towards the lighted doorway where Markey was slowly coming down the slippery steps. He took off his overcoat and hat, tossed them off the path onto the snow. Then, sliding a little on the iced walk, he took a step forward.

At the first blow, they both slipped and fell heavily to the sidewalk, half rising then, and again pulled each other to the ground. They found a better foothold in the thin snow to the side of the walk and rushed at each other, both swinging wildly and pressing out the snow into a pasty mud underfoot.

The street was deserted, and except for their short tired gasps and the padded sound as one or the other slipped down into the slushy mud, they fought in silence, clearly defined to each other by the full moonlight as well as by the amber glow that shone out of the open door. Several times they both slipped down together, and then for a while the conflict threshed about wildly on the lawn.

For ten, fifteen, twenty minutes they fought there senselessly in the moonlight. They had both taken off coats and vests at some silently agreed upon interval and now their shirts dripped from their backs in wet pulpy shreds. Both were torn and bleeding and so exhausted that they could stand only when by their position they mutually supported each other – the impact, the mere effort of a blow, would send them both to their hands and knees.

But it was not weariness that ended the business, and the very meaninglessness of the fight was a reason for not stopping. They stopped because once when they were straining at each other on the ground, they heard a man's footsteps coming along the sidewalk. They had rolled somehow into the shadow, and when they heard these footsteps they stopped fighting, stopped moving, stopped breathing, lay huddled together like two boys playing Indian until the footsteps had passed. Then, staggering to their feet, they looked at each other like two drunken men.

'I'll be damned if I'm going on with this thing any more,' cried Markey thickly.

'I'm not going on any more, either,' said John Andros. 'I've had enough of this thing.'

Again they looked at each other, sulkily this time, as if each suspected the other of urging him to a renewal of the fight. Markey spat out a mouthful of blood from a cut lip; then he cursed softly, and picking up his coat and vest, shook off the snow from them in a surprised way, as if their comparative dampness was his only worry in the world.

'Want to come in and wash up?' he asked suddenly.

'No, thanks,' said John. 'I ought to be going home – my wife'll be worried.'

He too picked up his coat and vest and then his overcoat and hat. Soaking wet and dripping with perspiration, it seemed absurd that less than half an hour ago he had been wearing all these clothes.

'Well – good night,' he said hesitantly.

Suddenly they walked towards each other and shook hands. It was no perfunctory hand-shake: John Andros's arm went around Markey's shoulder, and he patted him softly on the back for a little while.

'No harm done,' he said brokenly.

'No – you?'

'No, no harm done.'

'Well,' said John Andros after a minute, 'I guess I'll say good night.'

Limping slightly and with his clothes over his arm, John Andros turned away. The moonlight was still bright as he left the dark patch of trampled ground and walked over the intervening lawn. Down at the station, half a mile away, he could hear the rumble of the seven o'clock train.

'But you must have been crazy,' cried Edith brokenly. 'I thought you were going to fix it all up there and shake hands. That's why I went away.'

'Did you want us to fix it up?'

'Of course not, I never want to see them again. But I thought of course that was what you were going to do.' She was touching the bruises on his neck and back with iodine as he sat placidly in a hot bath. 'I'm going to get the doctor,' she said insistently. 'You may be hurt internally.'

He shook his head. 'Not a chance,' he answered. 'I don't want this to get all over the town.'

'I don't understand yet how it all happened.'

'Neither do I.' He smiled grimly. 'I guess these baby parties are pretty rough affairs.'

'Well, one thing –' suggested Edith hopefully, 'I'm certainly glad we have beef steak in the house for tomorrow's dinner.'

'Why?'

'For your eye, of course. Do you know I came within an ace of ordering veal? Wasn't that the luckiest thing?'

Half an hour later, dressed except that his neck would accommodate no collar, John moved his limbs experimentally before the glass. 'I believe I'll get myself in better shape,' he said thoughtfully. 'I must be getting old.'

'You mean so that next time you can beat him?'

'I did beat him,' he announced. 'At least, I beat him as much as he beat me. And there isn't going to be any next time. Don't you go calling people common any more. If you get in any trouble, you just take your coat and go home. Understand?'

'Yes, dear,' she said meekly. 'I was very foolish and now I understand.'

Out in the hall, he paused abruptly by the baby's door.

'Is she asleep?'

'Sound asleep. But you can go in and peek at her – just to say good night.'

They tiptoed in and bent together over the bed. Little Ede, her cheeks flushed with health, her pink hands clasped tight together, was sleeping soundly in the cool, dark room. John reached over the railing of the bed and passed his hand lightly over the silken hair.

'She's asleep,' he murmured in a puzzled way.

'Naturally, after such an afternoon.'

'Miz Andros,' the coloured maid's stage whisper floated in from the hall. 'Mr and Miz Markey downstairs an' want to see you. Mr Markey he's all cut up in pieces, mam'n. His face look like a roast beef. An' Miz Markey she 'pear mighty mad.'

'Why, what incomparable nerve!' exclaimed Edith. 'Just tell them we're not home. I wouldn't go down for anything in the world.'

'You most certainly will.' John's voice was hard and set.

'What?'

'You'll go down right now, and, what's more, whatever that other woman does, you'll apologize for what you said this afternoon. After that you don't ever have to see her again.'

'Why – John, I can't.'

'You've got to. And just remember that she probably hated to come over here twice as much as you hate to go downstairs.'

'Aren't you coming? Do I have to go alone?'

'I'll be down – in just a minute.'

John Andros waited until she had closed the door behind her; then he reached over into the bed, and picking up his daughter, blankets and all, sat down in the rocking-chair holding her tightly in his arms. She moved a little, and he held his breath, but she was sleeping soundly, and in a moment she was resting quietly in the hollow of his elbow. Slowly he bent his head until his cheek was against her bright hair. 'Dear little girl,' he whispered. 'Dear little girl, dear little girl.'

John Andros knew at length what it was he had fought for so savagely that evening. He had it now, he possessed it forever, and for some time he sat there rocking very slowly to and fro in the darkness.

A Short Trip Home*

I was near her, for I had lingered behind in order to get the short walk with her from the living-room to the front door. That was a lot, for she had flowered suddenly and I, being a man and only a year older, hadn't flowered at all, had scarcely dared to come near her in the week we'd been home. Nor was I going to say anything in that walk of ten feet, or touch her; but I had a vague hope she'd do something, give a gay little performance of some sort, personal only in so far as we were alone together.

She had bewitchment suddenly in the twinkle of short hairs on her neck, in the sure, clear confidence that at about eighteen begins to deepen and sing in attractive American girls. The lamplight shopped in the yellow strands of her hair.

Already she was sliding into another world – the world of Joe Jelke and Jim Cathcart waiting for us now in the car. In another year she would pass beyond me forever.

As I waited, feeling the others outside in the snowy night, feeling the excitement of Christmas week and the excitement of Ellen here, blooming away, filling the room with 'sex appeal' – a wretched phrase to express a quality that isn't like that at all – a maid came in from the dining-room, spoke to Ellen quietly and handed her a note. Ellen read it and her eyes faded down, as when the current grows weak on rural circuits, and smouldered off into space. Then she gave me an odd look – in

*In a moment of hasty misjudgement a whole paragraph of description was lifted out of this tale where it originated, and properly belongs, and applied to quite a different character in a novel of mine. I have ventured none the less to leave it here, even at the risk of seeming to serve warmed-over fare.–F.S.F.

which I probably didn't show – and without a word, followed the maid into the dining-room and beyond. I sat turning over the pages of a magazine for a quarter of an hour.

Joe Jelke came in, red-faced from the cold, his white silk muffler gleaming at the neck of his fur coat. He was a senior at New Haven, I was a sophomore. He was prominent, a member of Scroll and Keys, and, in my eyes, very distinguished and handsome.

'Isn't Ellen coming?'

'I don't know,' I answered discreetly. 'She was all ready.'

'Ellen!' he called. 'Ellen!'

He had left the front door open behind him and a great cloud of frosty air rolled in from outside. He went half-way up the stairs – he was a familiar in the house – and called again, till Mrs Baker came to the banister and said that Ellen was below. Then the maid, a little excited, appeared in the dining-room door.

'Mr Jelke,' she called in a low voice.

Joe's face fell as he turned towards her, sensing bad news.

'Miss Ellen says for you to go to the party. She'll come later.'

'What's the matter?'

'She can't come now. She'll come later.'

He hesitated, confused. It was the last big dance of vacation, and he was mad about Ellen. He had tried to give her a ring for Christmas, and failing that, got her to accept a gold mesh bag that must have cost two hundred dollars. He wasn't the only one – there were three or four in the same wild condition, and all in the ten days she'd been home – but his chance came first, for he was rich and gracious and at that moment the 'desirable' boy of St Paul. To me it seemed impossible that she could prefer another, but the rumour was she'd described Joe as much too perfect. I suppose he lacked mystery for her, and when a man is up against that with a young girl who isn't thinking of the practical side of marriage yet – well –.

'She's in the kitchen,' Joe said angrily.

'No, she's not.' The maid was defiant and a little scared.

'She is.'

'She went out the back way, Mr Jelke.'

'I'm going to see.'

I followed him. The Swedish servants washing dishes looked up sideways at our approach and an interested crashing of pans marked our passage through. The storm door, unbolted, was flapping in the wind, and as we walked out into the snowy yard we saw the tail light of a car turn the corner at the end of the back alley.

'I'm going after her,' Joe said slowly. 'I don't understand this at all.'

I was too awed by the calamity to argue. We hurried to his car and drove in a fruitless, despairing zigzag all over the residence section, peering into every machine on the streets. It was half an hour before the futility of the affair began to dawn upon him – St Paul is a city of almost three hundred thousand people – and Jim Cathcart reminded him that we had another girl to stop for. Like a wounded animal he sank into a melancholy mass of fur in the corner, from which position he jerked upright every few minutes and waved himself backward and forward a little in protest and despair.

Jim's girl was ready and impatient, but after what had happened her impatience didn't seem important. She looked lovely though. That's one thing about Christmas vacation – the excitement of growth and change and adventure in foreign parts transforming the people you've known all your life. Joe Jelke was polite to her in a daze – he indulged in one burst of short, loud, harsh laughter by way of conversation – and we drove to the hotel.

The chauffeur approached it on the wrong side – the side on which the line of cars was not putting forth guests – and because of that we came suddenly upon Ellen Baker just getting out of a small coupé. Even before we came to a stop, Joe Jelke had jumped excitedly from the car.

Ellen turned towards us, a faintly distracted look – perhaps of surprise, but certainly not of alarm – in her face; in fact, she didn't seem very aware of us. Joe approached her with a stern, dignified, injured and, I thought, just exactly correct reproof in his expression. I followed.

Seated in the coupé – he had not dismounted to help Ellen out – was a hard thin-faced man of about thirty-five with an air of being scarred, and a slight sinister smile. His eyes were a sort of taunt to the whole human family – they were the eyes of an animal, sleepy and quiescent in the presence of another species. They were helpless yet brutal, unhopeful yet confident. It was as if they felt themselves powerless to originate activity, but infinitely capable of profiting by a single gesture of weakness in another.

Vaguely I placed him as one of the sort of men whom I had been conscious of from my earliest youth as 'hanging around' – leaning with one elbow on the counters of tobacco stores, watching, through heaven knows what small chink of the mind, the people who hurried in and out. Intimate to garages, where he had vague business conducted in undertones, to barber shops and to the lobbies of theatres – in such places, anyhow, I placed the type, if type it was, that he reminded me of. Sometimes his face bobbed up in one of Tad's more savage cartoons, and I had always from earliest boyhood thrown a nervous glance towards the dim borderland where he stood, and seen him watching me and despising me. Once, in a dream, he had taken a few steps towards me, jerking his head back and muttering 'Say, kid' in what was intended to be a reassuring voice, and I had broken for the door in terror. This was that sort of man.

Joe and Ellen faced each other silently; she seemed, as I have said, to be in a daze. It was cold, but she didn't notice that her coat had blown open; Joe reached out and pulled it together, and automatically she clutched it with her hand.

Suddenly the man in the coupé, who had been watching them silently, laughed. It was a bare laugh, done with the breath – just a noisy jerk of the head – but it was an insult if I had ever heard one; definite and not to be passed over. I wasn't surprised when Joe, who was quick tempered, turned to him angrily and said:

'What's your trouble?'

The man waited a moment, his eyes shifting and yet staring,

and always seeing. Then he laughed again in the same way. Ellen stirred uneasily.

'Who is this – this –' Joe's voice trembled with annoyance.

'Look out now,' said the man slowly.

Joe turned to me.

'Eddie, take Ellen and Catherine in, will you?' he said quickly. . . . 'Ellen, go with Eddie.'

'Look out now,' the man repeated.

Ellen made a little sound with her tongue and teeth, but she didn't resist when I took her arm and moved her towards the side door of the hotel. It struck me as odd that she should be so helpless, even to the point of acquiescing by her silence in this imminent trouble.

'Let it go, Joe!' I called back over my shoulder. 'Come inside!'

Ellen, pulling against my arm, hurried us on. As we were caught up into the swinging doors I had the impression that the man was getting out of his coupé.

Ten minutes later, as I waited for the girls outside the women's dressing-room, Joe Jelke and Jim Cathcart stepped out of the elevator. Joe was very white, his eyes were heavy and glazed, there was a trickle of dark blood on his forehead and on his white muffler. Jim had both their hats in his hand.

'He hit Joe with brass knuckles,' Jim said in a low voice. 'Joe was out cold for a minute or so. I wish you'd send a bell boy for some witch-hazel and court-plaster.'

It was late and the hall was deserted; brassy fragments of the dance below reached us as if heavy curtains were being blown aside and dropping back into place. When Ellen came out I took her directly downstairs. We avoided the receiving line and went into a dim room set with scraggly hotel palms where couples sometimes sat out during the dance; there I told her what had happened.

'It was Joe's own fault,' she said, surprisingly. 'I told him not to interfere.'

This wasn't true. She had said nothing, only uttered one curious little click of impatience.

'You ran out the back door and disappeared for almost an hour,' I protested. 'Then you turned up with a hard-looking customer who laughed in Joe's face.'

'A hard-looking customer,' she repeated, as if tasting the sound of the words.

'Well, wasn't he? Where on earth did you get hold of him, Ellen?'

'On the train,' she answered. Immediately she seemed to regret this admission. 'You'd better stay out of things that aren't your business, Eddie. You see what happened to Joe.'

Literally I gasped. To watch her, seated beside me, immaculately glowing, her body giving off wave after wave of freshness and delicacy – and to hear her talk like that.

'But that man's a thug!' I cried. 'No girl could be safe with him. He used brass knuckles on Joe – brass knuckles!'

'Is that pretty bad?'

She asked this as she might have asked such a question a few years ago. She looked at me at last and really wanted an answer; for a moment it was as if she were trying to recapture an attitude that had almost departed; then she hardened again. I say 'hardened', for I began to notice that when she was concerned with this man her eyelids fell a little, shutting other things – everything else – out of view.

That was a moment I might have said something, I suppose, but in spite of everything, I couldn't light into her. I was too much under the spell of her beauty and its success. I even began to find excuses for her – perhaps that man wasn't what he appeared to be; or perhaps – more romantically – she was involved with him against her will to shield some one else. At this point people began to drift into the room and come up to speak to us. We couldn't talk any more, so we went in and bowed to the chaperones. Then I gave her up to the bright restless sea of the dance, where she moved in an eddy of her own among the pleasant islands of coloured favours set out on tables and the south winds from the brasses moaning across the hall. After a while I saw Joe Jelke sitting in a corner with a strip of court-plaster on his forehead watching Ellen as if she herself had struck him down, but I didn't go up to him. I felt queer myself – like I feel when I wake up after sleeping through an afternoon, strange and portentous, as if something had gone on in the interval that changed the values of everything and that I didn't see.

The night slipped on through successive phases of cardboard horns, amateur tableaux and flashlights for the morning papers. Then was the grand march and supper, and about two o'clock some of the committee dressed up as revenue agents pinched the party, and a facetious newspaper was distributed, burlesquing the events of the evening. And all the time out of the corner of my eye I watched the shining orchid on Ellen's shoulder as it moved like Stuart's plume about the room. I watched it with a definite foreboding until the last sleepy groups had crowded into the elevators, and then, bundled to the eyes in great shapeless fur coats, drifted out into the clear dry Minnesota night.

2

There is a sloping mid-section of our city which lies between the residence quarter on the hill and the business district on the level of the river. It is a vague part of town, broken by its climb into triangles and odd shapes – there are names like Seven Corners – and I don't believe a dozen people could draw an accurate map of it, though every one traversed it by trolley, auto or shoe leather twice a day. And though it was a busy section, it would be hard for me to name the business that comprised its activity. There were always long lines of trolley cars waiting to start somewhere; there was a big movie theatre and many small ones with posters of Hoot Gibson and Wonder Dogs and Wonder Horses outside; there were small stores with 'Old King Brady' and 'The Liberty Boys of '76' in the windows, and marbles, cigarettes and candy inside; and – one definite place at least – a fancy costumer whom we all visited at least once a year. Some time during boyhood I became aware that on one side of a certain obscure street there were bawdy houses, and all through the district were pawnshops, cheap jewellers, small athletic clubs and gymnasiums and somewhat too blatantly run-down saloons.

The morning after the Cotillion Club party, I woke up late and lazy, with the happy feeling that for a day or two more there was no chapel, no classes – nothing to do but wait for another party tonight. It was crisp and bright – one of those days when you forget how cold it is until your cheek freezes – and the events of the evening before seemed dim and far away. After luncheon I started down-town on foot through a light, pleasant snow of small flakes that would probably fall all afternoon, and I was about half through that halfway section of town – so far as I know, there's no inclusive name for it – when suddenly whatever idle thought was in my mind blew away like a hat and I began thinking hard of Ellen Baker. I began worrying about her as I'd never worried about anything outside myself before. I began to loiter, with an instinct to go up on the hill again and find her and talk to her; then I remembered that she was at a tea, and I went on again, but still thinking of her, and harder than ever. Right then the affair opened up again.

It was snowing, I said, and it was four o'clock on a December afternoon, when there is a promise of darkness in the air and the street lamps are just going on. I passed a combination pool parlour and restaurant, with a stove loaded with hot-dogs in the window, and a few loungers hanging around the door. The lights were on inside – not bright lights but just a few pale yellow high up on the ceiling – and the glow they threw out into the frosty dusk wasn't bright enough to tempt you to stare inside. As I went past, thinking hard of Ellen all this time, I took in the quartet of loafers out of the corner of my eye. I hadn't gone half a dozen steps down the street when one of them called to me, not by name but in a way clearly intended for my ear. I thought it was a tribute to my raccoon coat and paid no attention, but a moment later whoever it was called to me again in a peremptory voice. I was annoyed and turned around. There, standing in the group not ten feet away and looking at me with the half-sneer on his face with which he'd looked at Joe Jelke, was the scarred, thin-faced man of the night before.

He had on a black fancy-cut coat, buttoned up to his neck as if he were cold. His hands were deep in his pockets and he wore a derby and high button shoes. I was startled, and for a moment I hesitated, but I was most of all angry, and knowing that I was quicker with my hands than Joe Jelke, I took a tentative step back towards him. The other men weren't looking at me – I don't think they saw me at all – but I knew that this one recognized me; there was nothing casual about his look, no mistake.

'Here I am. What are you going to do about it?' his eyes seemed to say.

I took another step towards him and he laughed soundlessly, but with active contempt, and drew back into the group. I followed. I was going to speak to him – I wasn't sure what I was going to say – but when I came up he had either changed his mind and backed off, or else he wanted me to follow him inside, for he had slipped off and the three men watched my intent approach without curiosity. They were the same kind – sporty, but, unlike him, smooth rather than truculent; I didn't find any personal malice in their collective glance.

'Did he go inside?' I asked.

They looked at one another in that cagey way; a wink passed between them, and after a perceptible pause, one said:

'Who go inside?'

'I don't know his name.'

There was another wink. Annoyed and determined, I walked past them and into the pool room. There were a few people at a lunch counter along one side and a few more playing billiards, but he was not among them.

Again I hesitated. If his idea was to lead me into any blind part of the establishment – there were some half-open doors farther back – I wanted more support. I went up to the man at the desk.

'What became of the fellow who just walked in here?'

Was he on his guard immediately, or was that my imagination?

'What fellow?'

'Thin face – derby hat.'

'How long ago?'

'Oh – a minute.'

He shook his head again. 'Didn't see him,' he said.

I waited. The three men from outside had come in and were lined up beside me at the counter. I felt that all of them were looking at me in a peculiar way. Feeling helpless and increasingly uneasy, I turned suddenly and went out. A little way down the street I turned again and took a good look at the place, so I'd know it and could find it again. On the next corner I broke impulsively into a run, found a taxicab in front of the hotel and drove back up the hill.

Ellen wasn't home. Mrs Baker came downstairs and talked to me. She seemed entirely cheerful and proud of Ellen's beauty, and ignorant of anything amiss or of anything unusual having taken place the night before. She was glad that vacation was almost over – it was a strain and Ellen wasn't very strong. Then she said something that relieved my mind enormously. She was glad that I had come in, for of course Ellen would want to see me, and the time was so short. She was going back at half past eight tonight.

'Tonight!' I exclaimed. 'I thought it was the day after to-morrow.'

'She's going to visit the Brokaws in Chicago,' Mrs Baker said. 'They want her for some party. We just decided it today. She's leaving with the Ingersoll girls tonight.'

I was so glad I could barely restrain myself from shaking her hand. Ellen was safe. It had been nothing all along but a moment of the most casual adventure. I felt like an idiot, but I realized how much I cared about Ellen and how little I could endure anything terrible happening to her.

'She'll be in soon?'

'Any minute now. She just phoned from the University Club.'

I said I'd be over later – I lived almost next door and I

wanted to be alone. Outside I remembered I didn't have a key,
so I started up the Bakers' driveway to take the old cut we used
in childhood through the intervening yard. It was still snowing,
but the flakes were bigger now against the darkness, and trying
to locate the buried walk I noticed that the Bakers' back door
was ajar.

I scarcely know why I turned and walked into that kitchen.
There was a time when I would have known the Bakers' servants by name. That wasn't true now, but they knew me, and
I was aware of a sudden suspension as I came in – not only a
suspension of talk but of some mood of expectation that had
filled them. They began to go to work too quickly; they made
unnecessary movements and clamour – those three. The parlour maid looked at me in a frightened way and I suddenly
guessed she was waiting to deliver another message. I beckoned her into the pantry.

'I know all about this,' I said. 'It's a very serious business.
Shall I go to Mrs Baker now, or will you shut and lock that
back door?'

'Don't tell Mrs Baker, Mr Stinson!'

'Then I don't want Miss Ellen disturbed. If she is – and if she
is I'll know of it –' I delivered some outrageous threat about
going to all the employment agencies and seeing she never got
another job in the city. She was thoroughly intimidated when
I went out; it wasn't a minute before the back door was locked
and bolted behind me.

Simultaneously I heard a big car drive up in front, chains
crunching on the soft snow; it was bringing Ellen home, and I
went in to say good-bye.

Joe Jelke and two other boys were along, and none of the
three could manage to take his eyes off her, even to say hello
to me. She had one of those exquisite rose skins frequent in our
part of the country, and beautiful until the little veins begin to
break at about forty; now, flushed with the cold, it was a riot
of lovely delicate pinks like many carnations. She and Joe had
reached some sort of reconciliation, or at least he was too far
gone in love to remember last night; but I saw that though she

laughed a lot she wasn't really paying any attention to him or any of them. She wanted them to go, so that there'd be a message from the kitchen, but I knew that the message wasn't coming – that she was safe. There was talk of the Pump and Slipper dance at New Haven and of the Princeton Prom, and then, in various moods, we four left and separated quickly outside. I walked home with a certain depression of spirit and lay for an hour in a hot bath thinking that vacation was all over for me now that she was gone; feeling, even more deeply than I had yesterday, that she was out of my life.

And something eluded me, some one more thing to do, something that I had lost amid the events of the afternoon, promising myself to go back and pick it up, only to find that it had escaped me. I associated it vaguely with Mrs Baker, and now I seemed to recall that it had poked up its head somewhere in the stream of conversation with her. In my relief about Ellen I had forgotten to ask her a question regarding something she had said.

The Brokaws – that was it – where Ellen was to visit. I knew Bill Brokaw well; he was in my class at Yale. Then I remembered and sat bolt upright in the tub – the Brokaws weren't in Chicago this Christmas, they were at Palm Beach!

Dripping I sprang out of the tub, threw an insufficient union suit around my shoulders and sprang for the phone in my room. I got the connexion quick, but Miss Ellen had already started for the train.

Luckily our car was in, and while I squirmed, still damp, into my clothes, the chauffeur brought it around to the door. The night was cold and dry, and we made good time to the station through the hard, crusty snow. I felt queer and insecure starting out this way, but somehow more confident as the station loomed up bright and new against the dark, cold air. For fifty years my family had owned the land on which it was built and that made my temerity seem all right somehow. There was always a possibility that I was rushing in where angels feared to tread, but that sense of having a solid foothold in the past made me willing to make a fool of myself. This business was all wrong – terribly wrong. Any idea I had entertained that it was harmless dropped away now; between Ellen and some vague overwhelming catastrophe there stood me, or else the police and a scandal. I'm no moralist – there was another element here, dark and frightening, and I didn't want Ellen to go through it alone.

There are three competing trains from St Paul to Chicago that all leave within a few minutes of half past eight. Hers was the Burlington, and as I ran across the station I saw the grating being pulled over and the light above it go out. I knew, though, that she had a drawing-room with the Ingersoll girls, because her mother had mentioned buying the ticket, so she was, literally speaking, tucked in until tomorrow.

The C., M. & St P. gate was down at the other end and I raced for it and made it. I had forgotten one thing, though, and that was enough to keep me awake and worried half the night. This train got into Chicago ten minutes after the other. Ellen had that much time to disappear into one of the largest cities in the world.

I gave the porter a wire to my family to send from Milwaukee, and at eight o'clock next morning I pushed violently by a whole line of passengers, clamouring over their bags parked in the vestibule, and shot out of the door with a sort of scramble over the porter's back. For a moment the confusion of a great station, the voluminous sounds and echoes and cross-currents of bells and smoke struck me helpless. Then I dashed for the exit and towards the only chance I knew of finding her.

I had guessed right. She was standing at the telegraph counter, sending off heaven knows what black lie to her mother, and her expression when she saw me had a sort of terror mixed up with its surprise. There was cunning in it too. She was thinking quickly – she would have liked to walk away from me as if I weren't there, and go about her own business, but she couldn't. I was too matter-of-fact a thing in her life. So we stood silently watching each other and each thinking hard.

'The Brokaws are in Florida,' I said after a minute.

'It was nice of you to take such a long trip to tell me that.'

'Since you've found it out, don't you think you'd better go on to school?'

'Please let me alone, Eddie,' she said.

'I'll go as far as New York with you. I've decided to go back early myself.'

'You'd better let me alone.' Her lovely eyes narrowed and her face took on a look of dumb-animal resistance. She made a visible effort, the cunning flickered back into it, then both were gone, and in their stead was a cheerful reassuring smile that all but convinced me.

'Eddie, you silly child, don't you think I'm old enough to take care of myself?' I didn't answer. 'I'm going to meet a man, you understand. I just want to see him today. I've got my ticket East on the five o'clock train. If you don't believe it, here it is in my bag.'

'I believe you.'

'The man isn't anybody that you know and – frankly, I think you're being awfully fresh and impossible.'

'I know who the man is.'

Again she lost control of her face. The terrible expression came back into it and she spoke with almost a snarl:

'You'd better let me alone.'

I took the blank out of her hand and wrote out an explanatory telegram to her mother. Then I turned to Ellen and said a little roughly:

'We'll take the five o'clock train East together. Meanwhile you're going to spend the day with me.'

The mere sound of my own voice saying this so emphatically encouraged me, and I think it impressed her too; at any rate, she submitted – at least temporarily – and came along without protest while I bought my ticket.

When I start to piece together the fragments of that day a sort of confusion begins, as if my memory didn't want to yield up any of it, or my consciousness let any of it pass through. There was a bright, fierce morning during which we rode about in a taxicab and went to a department store where Ellen said she wanted to buy something and then tried to slip away from me by a back way. I had the feeling, for an hour, that someone was following us along Lake Shore Drive in a taxicab, and I would try to catch them by turning quickly or looking suddenly into the chauffeur's mirror; but I could find no one, and when I turned back I could see that Ellen's face was contorted with mirthless, unnatural laughter.

All morning there was a raw, bleak wind off the lake, but when we went to the Blackstone for lunch a light snow came down past the windows and we talked almost naturally about our friends, and about casual things. Suddenly her tone changed; she grew serious and looked me in the eye, straight and sincere.

'Eddie, you're the oldest friend I have,' she said, 'and you oughtn't to find it too hard to trust me. If I promise you faithfully on my word of honour to catch that five o'clock train, will you let me alone a few hours this afternoon?'

'Why?'

'Well' – she hesitated and hung her head a little – 'I guess everybody has a right to say – good-bye.'

'You want to say good-bye to that –'

'Yes, yes,' she said hastily; 'just a few hours, Eddie, and I promise faithfully that I'll be on that train.'

'Well, I suppose no great harm could be done in two hours. If you really want to say good-bye –'

I looked up suddenly, and surprised a look of such tense cunning in her face that I winced before it. Her lip was curled up and her eyes were slits again; there wasn't the faintest touch of fairness and sincerity in her whole face.

We argued. The argument was vague on her part and somewhat hard and reticent on mine. I wasn't going to be cajoled again into any weakness or be infected with any – and there was a contagion of evil in the air. She kept trying to imply, without any convincing evidence to bring forward, that everything was all right. Yet she was too full of the thing itself – whatever it was – to build up a real story, and she wanted to catch at any credulous and acquiescent train of thought that might start in my head, and work that for all it was worth. After every reassuring suggestion she threw out, she stared at me eagerly, as if she hoped I'd launch into a comfortable moral lecture with the customary sweet at the end – which in this case would be her liberty. But I was wearing her away a little. Two or three times it needed just a touch of pressure to bring her to the point of tears – which, of course, was what I wanted – but I couldn't seem to manage it. Almost I had her – almost possessed her interior attention – then she would slip away.

I bullied her remorselessly into a taxi about four o'clock and started for the station. The wind was raw again, with a sting of snow in it, and the people in the streets, waiting for buses and street cars too small to take them all in, looked cold and disturbed and unhappy. I tried to think how lucky we were to be comfortably off and taken care of, but all the warm, respectable world I had been part of yesterday had dropped away from me. There was something we carried with us now that was the enemy and the opposite of all that; it was in the cabs beside us, the streets we passed through. With a touch of panic, I wondered if I wasn't slipping almost imperceptibly into Ellen's attitude of mind. The column of passengers waiting to go aboard the train were as remote from me as people from another world, but it was I that was drifting away and leaving them behind.

My lower was in the same car with her compartment. It was an old-fashioned car, its lights somewhat dim, its carpets and upholstery full of the dust of another generation. There were half a dozen other travellers, but they made no special impression on me, except that they shared the unreality that I was beginning to feel everywhere around me. We went into Ellen's compartment, shut the door and sat down.

Suddenly I put my arms around her and drew her over to me, just as tenderly as I knew how – as if she were a little girl – as she was. She resisted a little, but after a moment she submitted and lay tense and rigid in my arms.

'Ellen,' I said helplessly, 'you asked me to trust you. You

have much more reason to trust me. Wouldn't it help to get rid of all this, if you told me a little?'

'I can't,' she said, very low – 'I mean, there's nothing to tell.'

'You met this man on the train coming home and you fell in love with him, isn't that true?'

'I don't know.'

'Tell me, Ellen. You fell in love with him?'

'I don't know. Please let me alone.'

'Call it anything you want,' I went on, 'he has some sort of hold over you. He's trying to use you; he's trying to get something from you. He's not in love with you.'

'What does that matter?' she said in a weak voice.

'It does matter. Instead of trying to fight this – this thing – you're trying to fight me. And I love you, Ellen. Do you hear? I'm telling you all of a sudden, but it isn't new with me. I love you.'

She looked at me with a sneer on her gentle face; it was an expression I had seen on men who were tight and didn't want to be taken home. But it was human. I was reaching her, faintly and from far away, but more than before.

'Ellen, I want you to answer me one question. Is he going to be on this train?'

She hesitated; then, an instant too late, she shook her head.

'Be careful, Ellen. Now I'm going to ask you one thing more, and I wish you'd try very hard to answer. Coming West, when did this man get on the train?'

'I don't know,' she said with an effort.

Just at that moment I became aware, with the unquestionable knowledge reserved for facts, that he was just outside the door. She knew it, too; the blood left her face and that expression of low-animal perspicacity came creeping back. I lowered my face into my hands and tried to think.

We must have sat there, with scarcely a word, for well over an hour. I was conscious that the lights of Chicago, then of Englewood and of endless suburbs, were moving by, and then there were no more lights and we were out on the dark flatness of Illinois. The train seemed to draw in upon itself; it took on the air of being alone. The porter knocked at the door and asked if he could make up the berth, but I said no and he went away.

After a while I convinced myself that the struggle inevitably coming wasn't beyond what remained of my sanity, my faith in the essential all-rightness of things and people. That this person's purpose was what we call 'criminal' I took for granted, but there was no need of ascribing to him an intelligence that belonged to a higher plane of human, or inhuman endeavour. It was still as a man that I considered him, and tried to get at his essence, his self-interest – what took the place in him of a comprehensible heart – but I suppose I more than half knew what I would find when I opened the door.

When I stood up Ellen didn't seem to see me at all. She was hunched into a corner staring straight ahead with a sort of film over her eyes, as if she were in a state of suspended animation of body and mind. I lifted her and put two pillows under her head and threw my fur coat over her knees. Then I knelt beside her and kissed her two hands, opened the door and went out into the hall.

I closed the door behind me and stood with my back against it for a minute. The car was dark save for the corridor lights at each end. There was no sound except the groaning of the couplers, the even click-a-click of the rails and someone's loud sleeping breath farther down the car. I became aware after a moment that the figure of a man was standing by the water cooler just outside the men's smoking-room, his derby hat on his head, his coat collar turned up around his neck as if he were cold, his hands in his coat pockets. When I saw him, he turned and went into the smoking-room, and I followed. He was sitting in the far corner of the long leather bench; I took the single armchair beside the door.

As I went in I nodded to him and he acknowledged my presence with one of those terrible soundless laughs of his. But this time it was prolonged, it seemed to go on forever, and mostly to cut it short, I asked: 'Where are you from?' in a voice I tried to make casual.

He stopped laughing and looked at me narrowly, wondering

what my game was. When he decided to answer, his voice was muffled as though he were speaking through a silk scarf, and it seemed to come from a long way off.

'I'm from St Paul, Jack.'

'Been making a trip home?'

He nodded. Then he took a long breath and spoke in a hard, menacing voice:

'You better get off at Fort Wayne, Jack.'

He was dead. He was dead as hell – he had been dead all along, but what force had flowed through him, like blood in his veins, out to St Paul and back, was leaving him now. A new outline – the outline of him dead – was coming through the palpable figure that had knocked down Joe Jelke.

He spoke again, with a sort of jerking effort:

'You get off at Fort Wayne, Jack, or I'm going to wipe you out.' He moved his hand in his coat pocket and showed me the outline of a revolver.

I shook my head. 'You can't touch me,' I answered. 'You see, I know.' His terrible eyes shifted over me quickly, trying to determine whether or not I did know. Then he gave a snarl and made as though he were going to jump to his feet.

'You climb off here or else I'm going to get you, Jack!' he cried hoarsely. The train was slowing up for Fort Wayne and his voice rang loud in the comparative quiet, but he didn't move from his chair – he was too weak, I think – and we sat staring at each other while workmen passed up and down outside the window banging the brakes and wheels, and the engine gave out loud mournful pants up ahead. No one got into our car. After a while the porter closed the vestibule door and passed back along the corridor, and we slid out of the murky yellow station light and into the long darkness.

What I remember next must have extended over a space of five or six hours, though it comes back to me as something without any existence in time – something that might have taken five minutes or a year. There began a slow, calculated assault on me, wordless and terrible. I felt what I can only call a strangeness stealing over me – akin to the strangeness I had felt all afternoon, but deeper and more intensified. It was like nothing so much as the sensation of drifting away, and I gripped the arms of the chair convulsively, as if to hang onto a piece in the living world. Sometimes I felt myself going out with a rush. There would be almost a warm relief about it, a sense of not caring; then, with a violent wrench of the will, I'd pull myself back into the room.

Suddenly I realized that from a while back I had stopped hating him, stopped feeling violently alien to him, and with the realization, I went cold and sweat broke out all over my head. He was getting around my abhorrence, as he had got around Ellen coming West on the train; and it was just that strength he drew from preying on people that had brought him up to the point of concrete violence in St Paul, and that, fading and flickering out, still kept him fighting now.

He must have seen that faltering in my heart, for he spoke at once, in a low, even, almost gentle voice: 'You better go now.'

'Oh, I'm not going,' I forced myself to say.

'Suit yourself, Jack.'

He was my friend, he implied. He knew how it was with me and he wanted to help. He pitied me. I'd better go away before it was too late. The rhythm of his attack was soothing as a song: I'd better go away – *and let him get at Ellen*. With a little cry I sat bolt upright.

'What do you want of this girl?' I said, my voice shaking.

'To make a sort of walking hell of her.'

His glance held a quality of dumb surprise, as if I were punishing an animal for a fault of which he was not conscious. For an instant I faltered; then I went on blindly:

'You've lost her; she's put her trust in me.'

His countenance went suddenly black with evil, and he cried: 'You're a liar!' in a voice that was like cold hands.

'She trusts me,' I said .'You can't touch her. She's safe!'

He controlled himself. His face grew bland, and I felt that curious weakness and indifference begin again inside me. What was the use of all this? What was the use?

'You haven't got much time left,' I forced myself to say, and then, in a flash of intuition, I jumped at the truth. 'You died, or you were killed, not far from here!' – Then I saw what I had not seen before – that his forehead was drilled with a small round hole like a larger picture nail leaves when it's pulled from a plaster wall. 'And now you're sinking. You've only a got a few hours. The trip home is over!'

His face contorted, lost all semblance of humanity, living or dead. Simultaneously the room was full of cold air and with a noise that was something between a paroxysm of coughing and a burst of horrible laughter, he was on his feet, reeking of shame and blasphemy.

'Come and look!' he cried. 'I'll show you –'

He took a step towards me, then another and it was exactly as if a door stood open behind him, a door yawning out to an inconceivable abyss of darkness and corruption. There was a scream of mortal agony, from him or from somewhere behind, and abruptly the strength went out of him in a long husky sigh and he wilted to the floor. . . .

How long I sat there, dazed with terror and exhaustion, I don't know. The next thing I remember is the sleepy porter shining shoes across the room from me, and outside the window the steel fires of Pittsburgh breaking the flat perspective of the night. There was something extended on the bench also – something too faint for a man, too heavy for a shadow. Even as I perceived it it faded off and away.

Some minutes later I opened the door of Ellen's compartment. She was asleep where I had left her. Her lovely cheeks were white and wan, but she lay naturally – her hands relaxed and her breathing regular and clear. What had possessed her had gone out of her, leaving her exhausted but her own dear self again.

I made her a little more comfortable, tucked a blanket around her, extinguished the light and went out.

3

When I came home for Easter vacation, almost my first act was to go down to the billiard parlour near Seven Corners. The man at the cash register quite naturally didn't remember my hurried visit of three months before.

'I'm trying to locate a certain party who, I think, came here a lot some time ago.'

I described the man rather accurately, and when I had finished, the cashier called to a little jockeylike fellow who was sitting near with an air of having something very important to do that he couldn't quite remember.

'Hey, Shorty, talk to this guy, will you? I think he's looking for Joe Varland.'

The little man gave me a tribal look of suspicion. I went and sat near him.

'Joe Varland's dead, fella,' he said grudgingly. 'He died last winter.'

I described him again – his overcoat, his laugh, the habitual expression of his eyes.

'That's Joe Varland you're looking for all right, but he's dead.'

'I want to find out something about him.'

'What you want to find out?'

'What did he do, for instance?'

'How should I know?'

'Look here! I'm not a policeman. I just want some kind of information about his habits. He's dead now and it can't hurt him. And it won't go beyond me.'

'Well' – he hesitated, looking me over – 'he was a great one for travelling. He got in a row in the station in Pittsburgh and a dick got him.'

I nodded. Broken pieces of the puzzle began to assemble in my head.

'Why was he a lot on trains?'

'How should I know, fella?'

'If you can use ten dollars, I'd like to know anything you may have heard on the subject.'

'Well,' said Shorty reluctantly, 'all I know is they used to say he worked the trains.'

'Worked the trains?'

'He had some racket of his own he'd never loosen up about. He used to work the girls travelling alone on the trains. Nobody ever knew much about it – he was a pretty smooth guy – but sometimes he'd turn up here with a lot of dough and he let 'em know it was the janes he got it off of.'

I thanked him and gave him the ten dollars and went out, very thoughtful, without mentioning that part of Joe Varland had made a last trip home.

Ellen wasn't West for Easter, and even if she had been I wouldn't have gone to her with the information, either – at least I've seen her almost every day this summer and we've managed to talk about everything else. Sometimes, though, she gets silent about nothing and wants to be very close to me, and I know what's in her mind.

Of course she's coming out this fall, and I have two more years at New Haven; still, things don't look so impossible as they did a few months ago. She belongs to me in a way – even if I lose her she belongs to me. Who knows? Anyhow, I'll always be there.

Magetism

I

The pleasant, ostentatious boulevard was lined at prosperous
intervals with New England Colonial houses – without ship
models in the hall. When the inhabitants moved out here the
ship models had at last been given to the children. The next
street was a complete exhibit of the Spanish-bungalow phase of
West Coast architecture; while two streets over, the cylindrical
windows and round towers of 1897 – melancholy antiques
which sheltered swamis, yogis, fortune tellers, dressmakers,
dancing teachers, art academies and chiropractors – looked
down now upon brisk buses and trolley cars. A little walk
around the block could, if you were feeling old that day, be a
discouraging affair.

On the green flanks of the modern boulevard children, with
their knees marked by the red stains of the mercurochrome
era, played with toys with a purpose – beams that taught engineering, soldiers that taught manliness, and dolls that taught
motherhood. When the dolls were so banged up that they stopped looking like real babies and began to look like dolls, the
children developed affection for them. Everything in the
vicinity – even the March sunlight – was new, fresh, hopeful and
thin, as you would expect in a city that had tripled its popula-
tion in fifteen years.

Among the very few domestics in sight that morning was a
handsome young maid sweeping the steps of the biggest house
on the street. She was a large, simple Mexican girl with the large,
simple ambitions of the time and the locality, and she was
already conscious of being a luxury – she received one hundred
dollars a month in return for her personal liberty. Sweeping,
Dolores kept an eye on the stairs inside, for Mr Hannaford's

car was waiting and he would soon be coming down to breakfast. The problem came first this morning, however – the problem as to whether it was a duty or a favour when she helped
the English nurse down the steps with the perambulator. The
English nurse always said 'Please', and 'Thanks very much',
but Dolores hated her and would have liked, without any
special excitement, to beat her insensible. Like most Latins
under the stimulus of American life, she had irresistible im-
pulses towards violence.

The nurse escaped, however. Her blue cape faded haughtily
into the distance just as Mr Hannaford, who had come quietly
downstairs, stepped into the space of the front door.

'Good morning.' He smiled at Dolores; he was young and
extraordinarily handsome. Dolores tripped on the broom and
fell off the stoop. George Hannaford hurried down the steps,
reached her as she was getting to her feet cursing volubly in
Mexican, just touched her arm with a helpful gesture and said,
'I hope you didn't hurt yourself.'

'Oh, no.'

'I'm afraid it was my fault; I'm afraid I startled you, coming
out like that.'

His voice had real regret in it; his brow was knit with solici-
tude.

'Are you sure you're all right ?'

'Aw, sure.'

'Didn't turn your ankle ?'

'Aw, no.'

'I'm terribly sorry about it.'

'Aw, it wasn't your fault.'

He was still frowning as she went inside, and Dolores, who
was not hurt and thought quickly, suddenly contemplated having a love affair with him. She looked at herself several times
in the pantry mirror and stood close to him as she poured his
coffee, but he read the paper and she saw that that was all for
the morning.

Hannaford entered his car and drove to Jules Rennard's
house. Jules was a French Canadian by birth, and George

Hannaford's best friend; they were fond of each other and spent much time together. Both of them were simple and dignified in their tastes and in their way of thinking, instinctively gentle, and in a world of the volatile and the bizarre found in each other a certain quiet solidity.

He found Jules at breakfast.

'I want to fish for barracuda,' said George abruptly. 'When will you be free? I want to take the boat and go down to Lower California.'

Jules had dark circles under his eyes. Yesterday he had closed out the greatest problem of his life by settling with his ex-wife for two hundred thousand dollars. He had married too young, and the former slavey from the Quebec slums had taken to drugs upon her failure to rise with him. Yesterday, in the presence of lawyers, her final gesture had been to smash his finger with the base of a telephone. He was tired of women for a while and welcomed the suggestion of a fishing trip.

'How's the baby?' he asked.

'The baby's fine.'

'And Kay?'

'Kay's not herself, but I don't pay any attention. What did you do to your hand?'

'I'll tell you another time. What's the matter with Kay, George?'

'Jealous.'

'Of who?'

'Helen Avery. It's nothing. She's not herself, that's all.' He got up. 'I'm late,' he said. 'Let me know as soon as you're free. Any time after Monday will suit me.'

George left and drove out by an interminable boulevard which narrowed into a long, winding concrete road and rose into the hilly country behind. Somewhere in the vast emptiness a group of buildings appeared, a barnlike structure, a row of offices, a large but quick restaurant and half a dozen small bungalows. The chauffeur dropped Hannaford at the main entrance. He went in and passed through various enclosures,

each marked off by swinging gates and inhabited by a stenographer.

'Is anybody with Mr Schroeder?' he asked, in front of a door
lettered with that name.

'No, Mr Hannaford.'

Simultaneously his eye fell on a young lady who was writing
at a desk aside, and he lingered a moment.

'Hello, Margaret,' he said. 'How are you, darling?'

A delicate, pale beauty looked up, frowning a little, still
abstracted in her work. It was Miss Donovan, the script girl, a
friend of many years.

'Hello. Oh, George, I didn't see you come in. Mr Douglas
wants to work on the book sequence this afternoon.'

'All right.'

'These are the changes we decided on Thursday night.' She
smiled up at him and George wondered for the thousandth
time why she had never gone into pictures.

'All right,' he said. 'Will initials do?'

'Your initials look like George Harris's.'

'Very well, darling.'

As he finished, Pete Schroeder opened his door and beckoned
him. 'George, come here!' he said with an air of excitement.
'I want you to listen to some one on the phone.'

Hannaford went in.

'Pick up the phone and say "Hello",' directed Schroeder.
'Don't say who you are.'

'Hello,' said Hannaford obediently.

'Who is this?' asked a girl's voice.

Hannaford put his hand over the mouthpiece. 'What am I
supposed to do?'

Schroeder snickered and Hannaford hesitated, smiling and
suspicious.

'Who do you want to speak to?' he temporized into the
phone.

'To George Hannaford, I want to speak to. Is this him?'

'Yes.'

'Oh, George; it's me.'

'Who?'

'Me – Gwen. I had an awful time finding you. They told me –'

'Gwen who?'

'Gwen – can't you hear? From San Francisco – last Thursday night.'

'I'm sorry,' objected George. 'Must be some mistake.'

'Is this George Hannaford?'

'Yes.'

The voice grew slightly tart: 'Well, this is Gwen Becker you spent last Thursday evening with in San Francisco. There's no use pretending you don't know who I am, because you do.'

Schroeder took the apparatus from George and hung up the receiver.

'Somebody has been doubling for me up in Frisco,' said Hannaford.

'So that's where you were Thursday night!'

'Those things aren't funny to me – not since that crazy Zeller girl. You can never convince them they've been sold because the man always looks something like you. What's new, Pete?'

'Let's go over to the stage and see.'

Together they walked out a back entrance, along a muddy walk, and opening a little door in the big blank wall of the studio building entered into its half darkness.

Here and there figures spotted the dim twilight, figures that turned up white faces to George Hannaford, like souls in purgatory watching the passage of a half-god through. Here and there were whispers and soft voices and, apparently from afar, the gentle tremolo of a small organ. Turning the corner made by some flats, they came upon the white crackling glow of a stage with two people motionless upon it.

An actor in evening clothes, his shirt front, collar and cuffs tinted a brilliant pink, made as though to get chairs for them, but they shook their heads and stood watching. For a long while nothing happened on the stage – no one moved. A row of lights went off with a savage hiss, went on again. The plaintive tap of a hammer begged admission to nowhere in the distance; a blue face appeared among the blinding lights above and called something unintelligible into the upper blackness. Then the silence was broken by a low clear voice from the stage:

'If you want to know why I haven't got stockings on, look in my dressing-room. I spoiled four pairs yesterday and two already this morning. . . . This dress weighs six pounds.'

A man stepped out of the group of observers and regarded the girl's brown legs; their lack of covering was scarcely distinguishable, but, in any event, her expression implied that she would do nothing about it. The lady was annoyed, and so intense was her personality that it had taken only a fractional flexing of her eyes to indicate the fact. She was a dark, pretty girl with a figure that would be full-blown sooner than she wished. She was just eighteen.

Had this been the week before, George Hannaford's heart would have stood still. Their relationship had been in just that stage. He hadn't said a word to Helen Avery that Kay could have objected to, but something had begun between them on the second day of this picture that Kay had felt in the air. Perhaps it had begun even earlier, for he had determined, when he saw Helen Avery's first release, that she should play opposite him. Helen Avery's voice and the dropping of her eyes when she finished speaking, like a sort of exercise in control, fascinated him. He had felt that they both tolerated something, that each knew half of some secret about people and life, and that if they rushed towards each other there would be a romantic communion of almost unbelievable intensity. It was this element of promise and possibility that had haunted him for a fortnight and was now dying away.

Hannaford was thirty, and he was a moving-picture actor only through a series of accidents. After a year in a small technical college he had taken a summer job with an electric company, and his first appearance in a studio was in the role of repairing a bank of Klieg lights. In an emergency he played a small part and made good, but for fully a year after that he thought of it as a purely transitory episode in his life. At first much of it had offended him – the almost hysterical egotism and excitability hidden under an extremely thin veil of elaborate good-fellowship. It was only recently, with the advent of such men as Jules Rennard into pictures, that he began to see the possibilities of a decent and secure private life, much as his would have been as a successful engineer. At last his success felt solid beneath his feet.

He met Kay Tomkins at the old Griffith Studios at Mamaroneck and their marriage was a fresh, personal affair, removed from most stage marriages. Afterwards they had possessed each other completely, had been pointed to: 'Look, there's one couple in pictures who manage to stay together.' It would have taken something out of many people's lives – people who enjoyed a vicarious security in the contemplation of their marriage – if they hadn't stayed together, and their love was fortified by a certain effort to live up to that.

He held women off by a polite simplicity that underneath was hard and watchful; when he felt a certain current being turned on he became emotionally stupid. Kay expected and took much more from men, but she, too, had a careful thermometer against her heart. Until the other night, when she reproached him for being interested in Helen Avery, there had been an absolute minimum of jealousy between them.

George Hannaford was still absorbed in the thought of Helen Avery as he left the studio and walked towards his bungalow over the way. There was in his mind, first, a horror that anyone should come between him and Kay, and second, a regret that he no longer carried that possibility in the forefront of his mind. It had given him a tremendous pleasure, like the things that had happened to him during his first big success, before he was so 'made' that there was scarcely anything better ahead; it was something to take out and look at – a new and still mysterious joy. It hadn't been love, for he was critical of Helen Avery as he had never been critical of Kay. But his feeling of last week had been sharply significant and memorable, and he was restless, now that it had passed.

Working that afternoon, they were seldom together, but he

was conscious of her and he knew that she was conscious of him.

She stood a long time with her back to him at one point, and when she turned at length, their eyes swept past each other's, brushing like bird wings. Simultaneously he saw they had gone far, in their way; it was well that he had drawn back. He was glad that someone came for her when the work was almost over.

Dressed, he returned to the office wing, stopping in for a moment to see Schroeder. No one answered his knock, and, turning the knob, he went in. Helen Avery was there alone.

Hannaford shut the door and they stared at each other. Her face was young, frightened. In a moment in which neither of them spoke, it was decided that they would have some of this out now. Almost thankfully he felt the warm sap of emotion flow out of his heart and course through his body.

'Helen!'

She murmured 'What?' in an awed voice.

'I feel terribly about this.' His voice was shaking.

Suddenly she began to cry; painful, audible sobs shook her. 'Have you got a handkerchief?' she said.

He gave her a handkerchief. At that moment there were steps outside. George opened the door halfway just in time to keep Schroeder from entering on the spectacle of her tears.

'Nobody's in,' he said facetiously. For a moment longer he kept his shoulder against the door. Then he let it open slowly.

Outside in his limousine, he wondered how soon Jules would be ready to go fishing.

2

From the age of twelve Kay Tompkins had worn men like rings on every finger. Her face was round, young, pretty and strong; a strength accentuated by the responsive play of brows and lashes around her clear, glossy, hazel eyes. She was the daughter of a senator from a Western state and she hunted unsuccessfully for glamour through a small Western city until she was seventeen, when she ran away from home and went on the stage. She was one of those people who are famous far beyond their actual achievement.

There was that excitement about her that seemed to reflect the excitement of the world. While she was playing small parts in Ziegfeld shows she attended proms at Yale, and during a temporary venture into pictures she met George Hannaford, already a star of the new 'natural' type then just coming into vogue. In him she found what she had been seeking.

She was at present in what is known as a dangerous state. For six months she had been helpless and dependent entirely upon George, and now that her son was the property of a strict and possessive English nurse, Kay, free again, suddenly felt the need of proving herself attractive. She wanted things to be as they had been before the baby was thought of. Also she felt that lately George had taken her too much for granted; she had a strong instinct that he was interested in Helen Avery.

When George Hannaford came home that night he had minimized to himself their quarrel of the previous evening and was honestly surprised at her perfunctory greeting.

'What's the matter, Kay?' he asked after a minute. 'Is this going to be another night like last night?'

'Do you know we're going out tonight?' she said, avoiding an answer.

'Where?'

'To Katherine Davis'. I didn't know whether you'd want to go –'

'I'd like to go.'

'I didn't know whether you'd want to go. Arthur Busch said he'd stop for me.'

They dined in silence. Without any secret thoughts to dip into like a child into a jam jar, George felt restless, and at the same time was aware that the atmosphere was full of jealousy, suspicion and anger. Until recently they had preserved between them something precious that made their house one of the pleasantest in Hollywood to enter. Now suddenly it might be any house; he felt common and he felt unstable. He had come near to making something bright and precious into something cheap and unkind. With a sudden surge of emotion, he crossed the room and was about to put his arm around her when the doorbell rang. A moment later Dolores announced Mr Arthur Busch.

Busch was an ugly, popular little man, a continuity writer and lately a director. A few years ago they had been hero and heroine to him, and even now, when he was a person of some consequence in the picture world, he accepted with equanimity Kay's use of him for such purposes as tonight's. He had been in love with her for years, but, because his love seemed hopeless, it had never caused him much distress.

They went on to the party. It was a housewarming, with Hawaiian musicians in attendance, and the guests were largely of the old crowd. People who had been in the early Griffith pictures, even though they were scarcely thirty, were considered to be of the old crowd; they were different from those coming along now, and they were conscious of it. They had a dignity and straightforwardness about them from the fact that they had worked in pictures before pictures were bathed in a golden haze of success. They were still rather humble before their amazing triumph, and thus, unlike the new generation, who took it all for granted, they were constantly in touch with reality. Half a dozen or so of the women were especially aware of being unique. No one had come along to fill their places; here and there a pretty face had caught the public imagination for a year, but those of the old crowd were already legends, ageless and disembodied. With all this, they were still young enough to believe that they would go forever.

George and Kay were greeted affectionately; people moved over and made place for them. The Hawaiians performed and the Duncan sisters sang at the piano. From the moment George saw who was here he guessed that Helen Avery would be here, too, and the fact annoyed him. It was not appropriate that she should be part of this gathering through which he and Kay had moved familiarly and tranquilly for years.

He saw her first when someone opened the swinging door

to the kitchen, and when, a little later, she came out and their eyes met, he knew absolutely that he didn't love her. He went up to speak to her, and at her first words he saw something had happened to her, too, that had dissipated the mood of the afternoon. She had got a big part.

'And I'm in a daze!' she cried happily. 'I didn't think there was a chance and I've thought of nothing else since I read the book a year ago.'

'It's wonderful. I'm awfully glad.'

He had the feeling, though, that he should look at her with a certain regret; one couldn't jump from such a scene as this afternoon to a plane of casual friendly interest. Suddenly she began to laugh.

'Oh, we're such actors, George – you and I.'

'What do you mean?'

'You know what I mean.'

'I don't.'

'Oh, yes, you do. You did this afternoon. It was a pity we didn't have a camera.'

Short of declaring then and there that he loved her, there was absolutely nothing more to say. He grinned acquiescently. A group formed around them and absorbed them, and George, feeling that the evening had settled something, began to think about going home. An excited and sentimental elderly lady – someone's mother – came up and began telling him how much she believed in him, and he was polite and charming to her, as only he could be, for half an hour. Then he went to Kay, who had been sitting with Arthur Busch all evening, and suggested that they go.

She looked up unwillingly. She had had several highballs and the fact was mildly apparent. She did not want to go, but she got up after a mild argument and George went upstairs for his coat. When he came down Katherine Davis told him that Kay had already gone out to the car.

The crowd had increased; to avoid a general good-night he went out through the sun-parlour door to the lawn; less than twenty feet away from him he saw the figures of Kay and

Arthur Busch against a bright street lamp; they were standing close together and staring into each other's eyes. He saw that they were holding hands.

After the first start of surprise George instinctively turned about, retraced his steps, hurried through the room he had just left, and came noisily out the front door. But Kay and Arthur Busch were still standing close together, and it was lingeringly and with abstracted eyes that they turned around finally and saw him. Then both of them seemed to make an effort; they drew apart as if it was a physical ordeal. George said good-bye to Arthur Busch with special cordiality, and in a moment he and Kay were driving homeward through the clear California night.

He said nothing, Kay said nothing. He was incredulous. He suspected that Kay had kissed a man here and there, but he had never seen it happen or given it any thought. This was different; there had been an element of tenderness in it and there was something veiled and remote in Kay's eyes that he had never seen there before.

Without having spoken, they entered the house; Kay stopped by the library door and looked in.

'There's someone there,' she said, and she added without interest: 'I'm going upstairs. Good night.'

As she ran up the stairs the person in the library stepped out into the hall.

'Mr Hannaford –'

He was a pale and hard young man; his face was vaguely familiar, but George didn't remember where he had seen it before.

'Mr Hannaford?' said the young man. 'I recognize you from your pictures.' He looked at George, obviously a little awed.

'What can I do for you?'

'Well, will you come in here?'

'What is it? I don't know who you are.'

'My name is Donovan. I'm Margaret Donovan's brother.' His face toughened a little.

'Is anything the matter?'

Donovan made a motion towards the door. 'Come in here.' His voice was confident now, almost threatening.

George hesitated, then he walked into the library. Donovan followed and stood across the table from him, his legs apart, his hands in his pockets.

'Hannaford,' he said, in the tone of a man trying to whip himself up to anger, 'Margaret wants fifty thousand dollars.'

'What the devil are you talking about?' exclaimed George incredulously.

'Margaret wants fifty thousand dollars,' repeated Donovan.

'You're Margaret Donovan's brother?'

'I am.'

'I don't believe it.' But he saw the resemblance now. 'Does Margaret know you're here?'

'She sent me here. She'll hand over those two letters for fifty thousand, and no questions asked.'

'What letters?' George chuckled irresistibly. 'This is some joke of Schroeder's, isn't it?'

'This ain't a joke, Hannaford. I mean the letters you signed your name to this afternoon.'

3

An hour later George went upstairs in a daze. The clumsiness of the affair was at once outrageous and astounding. That a friend of seven years should suddenly request his signature on papers that were not what they were purported to be made all his surroundings seem diaphanous and insecure. Even now the design engrossed him more than a defence against it, and he tried to re-create the steps by which Margaret had arrived at this act of recklessness or despair.

She had served as a script girl in various studios and for various directors for ten years; earning first twenty, now a hundred dollars a week. She was lovely-looking and she was intelligent; at any moment in those years she might have asked for a screen test, but some quality of initiative or ambition had been lacking. Not a few times had her opinion made or broken incipient careers. Still she waited at directors' elbows, increasingly aware that the years were slipping away.

That she had picked George as a victim amazed him most of all. Once, during the year before his marriage, there had been a momentary warmth; he had taken her to a Mayfair ball, and he remembered that he had kissed her going home that night in the car. The flirtation trailed along hesitatingly for a week. Before it could develop into anything serious he had gone East and met Kay.

Young Donovan had shown him a carbon of the letters he had signed. They were written on the typewriter that he kept in his bungalow at the studio, and they were carefully and convincingly worded. They purported to be love letters, asserting that he was Margaret Donovan's lover, that he wanted to marry her, and that for that reason he was about to arrange a divorce. It was incredible. Someone must have seen him sign them that morning; someone must have heard her say: 'Your initials are like Mr Harris's.'

George was tired. He was training for a screen football game to be played next week, with the Southern California varsity as extras, and he was used to regular hours. In the middle of a confused and despairing sequence of thought about Margaret Donovan and Kay, he suddenly yawned. Mechanically he went upstairs, undressed and got into bed.

Just before dawn Kay came to him in the garden. There was a river that flowed past it now, and boats faintly lit with green and yellow lights moved slowly, remotely by. A gentle starlight fell like rain upon the dark, sleeping face of the world, upon the black mysterious bosoms of the trees, the tranquil gleaming water and the farther shore.

The grass was damp, and Kay came to him on hurried feet; her thin slippers were drenched with dew. She stood upon his shoes, nestling close to him, and held up her face as one shows a book open at a page.

'Think how you love me,' she whispered. 'I don't ask you to love me always like this, but I ask you to remember.'

'You'll always be like this to me.'

'Oh, no; but promise me you'll remember.' Her tears were falling. 'I'll be different, but somewhere lost inside me there'll always be the person I am tonight.'

The scene dissolved slowly but George struggled into consciousness. He sat up in bed; it was morning. In the yard outside he heard the nurse instructing his son in the niceties of behaviour for two-month-old babies. From the yard next door a small boy shouted mysteriously: 'Who let that barrier through on me?'

Still in his pyjamas, George went to the phone and called his lawyers. Then he rang for his man, and while he was being shaved a certain order evolved from the chaos of the night before. First, he must deal with Margaret Donovan; second, he must keep the matter from Kay, who in her present state might believe anything; and third, he must fix things up with Kay. The last seemed the most important of all.

As he finished dressing he heard the phone ring downstairs and, with an instinct of danger, picked up the receiver.

'Hello.... Oh, yes.' Looking up, he saw that both his doors were closed. 'Good morning, Helen.... It's all right, Dolores. I'm taking it up here.' He waited till he heard the receiver click downstairs.

'How are you this morning, Helen?'

'George, I called up about last night. I can't tell you how sorry I am.'

'Sorry? Why are you sorry?'

'For treating you like that. I don't know what was in me, George. I didn't sleep all night thinking how terrible I'd been.'

A new disorder established itself in George's already littered mind.

'Don't be silly,' he said. To his despair he heard his own voice run on: 'For a minute I didn't understand, Helen. Then I thought it was better so.'

'Oh, George,' came her voice after a moment, very low.

Another silence. He began to put in a cuff button.

'I had to call up,' she said after a moment. 'I couldn't leave things like that.'

The cuff button dropped to the floor; he stooped to pick it up, and then said 'Helen!' urgently into the mouthpiece to cover the fact that he had momentarily been away.

'What, George?'

At this moment the hall door opened and Kay, radiating a faint distaste, came into the room. She hesitated.

'Are you busy?'

'It's all right.' He stared into the mouthpiece for a moment. 'Well, good-bye,' he muttered abruptly and hung up the receiver. He turned to Kay: 'Good morning.'

'I didn't mean to disturb you,' she said distantly.

'You didn't disturb me.' He hesitated. 'That was Helen Avery.'

'It doesn't concern me who it was. I came to ask you if we're going to the Coconut Grove tonight.'

'Sit down, Kay.'

'I don't want to talk.'

'Sit down a minute,' he said impatiently. She sat down. 'How long are you going to keep this up?' he demanded.

'I'm not keeping up anything. We're simply through, George, and you know it as well as I do.'

'That's absurd,' he said. 'Why, a week ago —'

'It doesn't matter. We've been getting nearer to this for months, and now it's over.'

'You mean you don't love me?' He was not particularly alarmed. They had been through scenes like this before.

'I don't know. I suppose I'll always love you in a way.' Suddenly she began to sob. 'Oh, it's all so sad. He's cared for me so long.'

George stared at her. Face to face with what was apparently a real emotion, he had no words of any kind. She was not angry, not threatening or pretending, not thinking about him at all, but concerned entirely with her emotions towards another man.

'What is it?' he cried. 'Are you trying to tell me you're in love with this man?'

'I don't know,' she said helplessly.

He took a step towards her, then went to the bed and lay down on it, staring in misery at the ceiling. After a while a maid knocked to say that Mr Busch and Mr Castle, George's lawyer, were below. The fact carried no meaning to him. Kay went into her room and he got up and followed her.

'Let's send word we're out,' he said. 'We can go away somewhere and talk this over.'

'I don't want to go away.'

She was already away, growing more mysterious and remote with every minute. The things on her dressing-table were the property of a stranger.

He began to speak in a dry, hurried voice. 'If you're still thinking about Helen Avery, it's nonsense. I've never given a damn for anybody but you.'

They went downstairs and into the living-room. It was nearly noon – another bright emotionless California day. George saw that Arthur Busch's ugly face in the sunshine was wan and white; he took a step towards George and then stopped, as if he were waiting for something – a challenge, a reproach, a blow.

In a flash the scene that would presently take place ran itself off in George's mind. He saw himself moving through the scene, saw his part, an infinite choice of parts, but in every one of them Kay would be against him and with Arthur Busch. And suddenly he rejected them all.

'I hope you'll excuse me,' he said quickly to Mr Castle. 'I called you up because a script girl named Margaret Donovan wants fifty thousand dollars for some letters she claims I wrote her. Of course the whole thing is –' He broke off. It didn't matter. 'I'll come to see you tomorrow.' He walked up to Kay and Arthur, so that only they could hear.

'I don't know about you two – what you want to do. But leave me out of it; you haven't any right to inflict any of it on me, for after all it's not my fault. I'm not going to be mixed up in your emotions.'

He turned and went out. His car was before the door and

he said 'Go to Santa Monica' because it was the first name that popped into his head. The car drove off into the everlasting hazeless sunlight.

He rode for three hours, past Santa Monica and then along towards Long Beach by another road. As if it were something he saw out of the corner of his eye and with but a fragment of his attention, he imagined Kay and Arthur Busch progressing through the afternoon. Kay would cry a great deal and the situation would seem harsh and unexpected to them at first, but the tender closing of the day would draw them together. They would turn inevitably towards each other and he would slip more and more into the position of the enemy outside.

Kay had wanted him to get down in the dirt and dust of a scene and scramble for her. Not he; he hated scenes. Once he stooped to compete with Arthur Busch in pulling at Kay's heart, he would never be the same to himself. He would always be a little like Arthur Busch; they would always have that in common, like a shameful secret. There was little of the theatre about George; the millions before whose eyes the moods and changes of his face had flickered during ten years had not been deceived about that. From the moment when, as a boy of twenty, his handsome eyes had gazed off into the imaginary distance of a Griffith Western, his audience had been really watching the progress of a straightforward, slow-thinking, romantic man through an accidentally glamorous life.

His fault was that he had felt safe too soon. He realized suddenly that the two Fairbankses, in sitting side by side at table, were not keeping up a pose. They were giving hostages to fate. This was perhaps the most bizarre community in the rich, wild, bored empire, and for a marriage to succeed here, you must expect nothing or you must be always together. For a moment his glance had wavered from Kay and he stumbled blindly into disaster.

As he was thinking this and wondering where he would go and what he should do, he passed an apartment house that jolted his memory. It was on the outskirts of town, a pink horror built to represent something, somewhere, so cheaply and sketchily that whatever it copied the architect must have long since forgotten. And suddenly George remembered that he had once called for Margaret Donovan here the night of a Mayfair dance.

'Stop at this apartment!' he called through the speaking-tube.

He went in. The negro elevator boy stared open-mouthed at him as they rose in the cage. Margaret Donovan herself opened the door.

When she saw him she shrank away with a little cry. As he entered and closed the door she retreated before him into the front room. George followed.

It was twilight outside and the apartment was dusky and sad. The last light fell softly on the standardized furniture and the great gallery of signed photographs of moving-picture people that covered one wall. Her face was white, and as she stared at him she began nervously wringing her hands.

'What's this nonsense, Margaret?' George said, trying to keep any reproach out of his voice. 'Do you need money that bad?'

She shook her head vaguely. Her eyes were still fixed on him with a sort of terror; George looked at the floor.

'I suppose this was your brother's idea. At least I can't believe you'd be so stupid.' He looked up, trying to preserve the brusque masterly attitude of one talking to a naughty child, but at the sight of her face every emotion except pity left him. 'I'm a little tired. Do you mind if I sit down?'

'No.'

'I'm a little confused today,' said George after a minute. 'People seem to have it in for me today.'

'Why, I thought' – her voice became ironic in mid-sentence – 'I thought everybody loved you, George.'

'They don't.'

'Only me?'

'Yes,' he said abstractedly.

'I wish it had been only me. But then, of course, you wouldn't have been you.'

Suddenly he realized that she meant what she was saying.

'That's just nonsense.'

'At least you're here,' Margaret went on. 'I suppose I ought to be glad of that. And I am. I most decidedly am. I've often thought of you sitting in that chair, just at this time when it was almost dark. I used to make up little one-act plays about what would happen then. Would you like to hear one of them? I'll have to begin by coming over and sitting on the floor at your feet.'

Annoyed and yet spellbound, George kept trying desperately to seize upon a word or mood that would turn the subject.

'I've seen you sitting there so often that you don't look a bit more real than your ghost. Except that your hat has squashed your beautiful hair down on one side and you've got dark circles or dirt under your eyes. You look white, too, George. Probably you were on a party last night.'

'I was. And I found your brother waiting for me when I got home.'

'He's a good waiter, George. He's just out of San Quentin prison, where he's been waiting the last six years.'

'Then it was his idea?'

'We cooked it up together. I was going to China on my share.'

'Why was I the victim?'

'That seemed to make it realer. Once I thought you were going to fall in love with me five years ago.'

The bravado suddenly melted out of her voice and it was still light enough to see that her mouth was quivering.

'I've loved you for years,' she said – 'since the first day you came West and walked into the old Realart Studio. You were so brave about people, George. Whoever it was, you walked right up to them and tore something aside as if it was in your way and began to know them. I tried to make love to you, just like the rest, but it was difficult. You drew people right up close to you and held them there, not able to move either way.'

'This is all entirely imaginary,' said George, frowning uncomfortably, 'and I can't control –'

'No, I know. You can't control charm. It's simply got to be used. You've got to keep your hand in if you have it, and go through life attaching people to you that you don't want. I don't blame you. If you only hadn't kissed me the night of the Mayfair dance. I suppose it was the champagne.'

George felt as if a band which had been playing for a long time in the distance had suddenly moved up and taken a station beneath his window. He had always been conscious that things like this were going on around him. Now that he thought of it, he had always been conscious that Margaret loved him, but the faint music of these emotions in his ear had seemed to bear no relation to actual life. They were phantoms that he had conjured up out of nothing; he had never imagined their actual incarnations. At his wish they should die inconsequently away.

'You can't imagine what it's been like,' Margaret continued after a minute. 'Things you've just said and forgotten, I've put myself asleep night after night remembering – trying to squeeze something more out of them. After that night you took me to the Mayfair other men didn't exist for me any more. And there were others, you know – lots of them. But I'd see you walking along somewhere about the lot, looking at the ground and smiling a little, as if something very amusing had just happened to you, the way you do. And I'd pass you and you'd look up and really smile: "Hello, darling!" "Hello, darling" and my heart would turn over. That would happen four times a day.'

George stood up and she, too, jumped up quickly.

'Oh, I've bored you,' she cried softly. 'I might have known I'd bore you. You want to go home. Let's see – is there anything else? Oh, yes; you might as well have those letters.'

Taking them out of a desk, she took them to a window and identified them by a rift of lamplight.

'They're really beautiful letters. They'd do you credit. I suppose it was pretty stupid, as you say, but it ought to teach you a lesson about – about signing things, or something.' She tore the letters small and threw them in the wastebasket: 'Now go on,' she said.

'Why must I go now?'

For the third time in twenty-four hours sad and uncontrollable tears confronted him.

'Please go!' she cried angrily – 'or stay if you like. I'm yours for the asking. You know it. You can have any woman you want in the world by just raising your hand. Would I amuse you?'

'Margaret –'

'Oh, go on then.' She sat down and turned her face away. 'After all you'll begin to look silly in a minute. You wouldn't like that, would you? So get out.'

George stood there helpless, trying to put himself in her place and say something that wouldn't be priggish, but nothing came.

He tried to force down his personal distress, his discomfort, his vague feeling of scorn, ignorant of the fact that she was watching him and understanding it all and loving the struggle in his face. Suddenly his own nerves gave way under the strain of the past twenty-four hours and he felt his eyes grow dim and his throat tighten. He shook his head helplessly. Then he turned away – still not knowing that she was watching him and loving him until she thought her heart would burst with it – and went out to the door.

4

The car stopped before his house, dark save for small lights in the nursery and the lower hall. He heard the telephone ringing, but when he answered it, inside, there was no one on the line. For a few minutes he wandered about in the darkness, moving from chair to chair and going to the window to stare out into the opposite emptiness of the night.

It was strange to be alone, to feel alone. In his overwrought condition the fact was not unpleasant. As the trouble of last night had made Helen Avery infinitely remote, so his talk with

Margaret had acted as a catharsis to his own personal misery. It would swing back upon him presently, he knew, but for a moment his mind was too tired to remember, to imagine or to care.

Half an hour passed. He saw Dolores issue from the kitchen, take the paper from the front steps and carry it back to the kitchen for a preliminary inspection. With a vague idea of packing his grip, he went upstairs. He opened the door of Kay's room and found her lying down.

For a moment he didn't speak, but moved around the bathroom between. Then he went into her room and switched on the lights.

'What's the matter?' he asked casually. 'Aren't you feeling well?'

'I've been trying to get some sleep,' she said. 'George, do you think that girl's gone crazy?'

'What girl?'

'Margaret Donovan. I've never heard of anything so terrible in my life.'

For a moment he thought that there had been some new development.

'Fifty thousand dollars!' she cried indignantly. 'Why, I wouldn't give it to her even if it were true. She ought to be sent to jail.'

'Oh, it's not so terrible as that,' he said. 'She has a brother who's a pretty bad egg and it was his idea.'

'She's capable of anything,' Kay said solemnly. 'And you're just a fool if you don't see it. I've never liked her. She has dirty hair.'

'Well, what of it?' he demanded impatiently, and added: 'Where's Arthur Busch?'

'He went home right after lunch. Or rather I sent him home.'

'You decided you were not in love with him?'

She looked up almost in surprise. 'In love with him? Oh, you mean this morning. I was just mad at you; you ought to have known that. I was a little sorry for him last night, but I guess it was the highballs.'

'Well, what did you mean when you –' He broke off. Wherever he turned he found a muddle, and he resolutely determined not to think.

'My heavens!' exclaimed Kay. 'Fifty thousand dollars!'

'Oh, drop it. She tore up the letters – she wrote them herself – and everything's all right.'

'George.'

'Yes.'

'Of course Douglas will fire her right away.'

'Of course he won't. He won't know anything about it.'

'You mean to say you're not going to let her go? After this?'

He jumped up. 'Do you suppose she thought that?' he cried.

'Thought what?'

'That I'd have them let her go?'

'You certainly ought to.'

He looked hastily through the phone book for her name.

'Oxford –' he called.

After an unusually long time the switchboard operator answered: 'Bourbon Apartments.'

'Miss Margaret Donovan, please.'

'Why –' The operator's voice broke off. 'If you'll just wait a minute, please.' He held the line; the minute passed, then another. Then the operator's voice: 'I couldn't talk to you then. Miss Donovan has had an accident. She's shot herself. When you called they were taking her through the lobby to St Catherine's Hospital.'

'Is she – is it serious?' George demanded frantically.

'They thought so at first, but now they think she'll be all right. They're going to probe for the bullet.'

'Thank you.'

He got up and turned to Kay.

'She's tried to kill herself,' he said in a strained voice. 'I'll have to go around to the hospital. I was pretty clumsy this afternoon and I think I'm partly responsible for this.'

'George,' said Kay suddenly.

'What?'

'Don't you think it's sort of unwise to get mixed up in this? People might say —'

'I don't give a damn what they say,' he answered roughly.

He went to his room and automatically began to prepare for going out. Catching sight of his face in the mirror, he closed his eyes with a sudden exclamation of distaste, and abandoned the intention of brushing his hair.

'George,' Kay called from the next room, 'I love you.'

'I love you too.'

'Jules Rennard called up. Something about barracuda fishing. Don't you think it would be fun to get up a party? Men and girls both?'

'Somehow the idea doesn't appeal to me. The whole idea of barracuda fishing —'

The phone rang below and he started. Dolores was answering it.

It was a lady who had already called twice today.

'Is Mr Hannaford in?'

'No,' said Dolores promptly. She stuck out her tongue and hung up the phone just as George Hannaford came downstairs. She helped him into his coat, standing as close as she could to him, opened the door and followed a little way out on the porch.

'Meester Hannaford,' she said suddenly, 'that Miss Avery she call up five-six times today. I tell her you out and say nothing to missus.'

'What?' He stared at her, wondering how much she knew about his affairs.

'She call up just now and I say you out.'

'All right,' he said absently.

'Meester Hannaford.'

'Yes, Dolores.'

'I deedn't hurt myself thees morning when I fell off the porch.'

'That's fine. Good night, Dolores.'

'Good night, Meester Hannaford.'

George smiled at her, faintly, fleetingly, tearing a veil from between them, unconsciously promising her a possible admission to the thousand delights and wonders that only he knew and could command. Then he went to his waiting car and Dolores, sitting down on the stoop, rubbed her hands together in a gesture that might have expressed either ecstasy or strangulation, and watched the rising of the thin, pale California moon.

The Rough Crossing

I

Once on the long, covered piers, you have come into a ghostly country that is no longer Here and not yet There. Especially at night. There is a hazy yellow vault full of shouting, echoing voices. There is the rumble of trucks and the clump of trunks, the strident chatter of a crane and the first salt smell of the sea. You hurry through, even though there's time. The past, the continent, is behind you; the future is that glowing mouth in the side of the ship; this dim turbulent alley is too confusedly the present.

Up the gangplank, and the vision of the world adjusts itself, narrows. One is a citizen of a commonwealth smaller than Andorra. One is no longer so sure of anything. Curiously unmoved the men at the purser's desk, cell-like the cabin, disdainful the eyes of voyagers and their friends, solemn the officer who stands on the deserted promenade deck thinking something of his own as he stares at the crowd below. A last odd idea that one didn't really have to come, then the loud, mournful whistles, and the thing – certainly not the boat, but rather a human idea, a frame of mind – pushes forth into the big dark night.

Adrian Smith, one of the celebrities on board – not a very great celebrity, but important enough to be bathed in flashlight by a photographer who had been given his name, but wasn't sure what his subject 'did' – Adrian Smith and his blonde wife, Eva, went up to the promenade deck, passed the melancholy ship's officer, and, finding a quiet aerie, put their elbows on the rail.

'We're going!' he cried presently, and they both laughed in ecstasy. 'We've escaped. They can't get us now.'

'Who?'

He waved his hand vaguely at the civic tiara.

'All those people out there. They'll come with their posses and their warrants and list of crimes we've committed, and ring the bell at our door on Park Avenue and ask for the Adrian Smiths, but what ho! the Adrian Smiths and their children and nurse are off for France.'

'You make me think we really have committed crimes.'

'They can't have you,' he said frowning. 'That's one thing they're after me about — they know I haven't got any right to a person like you, and they're furious. That's one reason I'm glad to get away.'

'Darling,' said Eva.

She was twenty-six — five years younger than he. She was something precious to everyone who knew her.

'I like this boat better than the *Majestic* or the *Aquitania*,' she remarked, unfaithful to the ships that had served their honeymoon.

'It's much smaller.'

'But it's very slick and it has all those little shops along the corridors. And I think the staterooms are bigger.'

'The people are very formal — did you notice? — as if they thought everyone else was a card sharp. And in about four days half of them will be calling the other half by their first names.'

Four of the people came by now — a quartet of young girls abreast, making a circuit of the deck. Their eight eyes swept momentarily towards Adrian and Eva, and then swept automatically back, save for one pair which lingered for an instant with a little start. They belonged to one of the girls in the middle, who was, indeed, the only passenger of the four. She was not more than eighteen — a dark little beauty with the fine crystal gloss over her that, in brunettes, takes the place of a blonde's bright glow.

'Now, who's that?' wondered Adrian. 'I've seen her before.'

'She's pretty,' said Eva.

'Yes.' He kept wondering, and Eva deferred momentarily

to his distraction; then, smiling up at him, she drew him back into their privacy.

'Tell me more,' she said.

'About what?'

'About us – what a good time we'll have, and how we'll be much better and happier, and very close always.'

'How could we be any closer?' His arm pulled her to him.

'But I mean never even quarrel any more about silly things. You know, I made up my mind when you gave me my birthday present last week' – her fingers caressed the fine seed pearls at her throat – 'that I'd try never to say a mean thing to you again.'

'You never have, my precious.'

Yet even as he strained her against his side he knew that the moment of utter isolation had passed almost before it had begun. His antennae were already out, feeling over this new world.

'Most of the people look rather awful,' he said – 'little and swarthy and ugly. Americans didn't use to look like that.'

'They look dreary,' she agreed. 'Let's not get to know anybody, but just stay together.'

A gong was beating now, and stewards were shouting down the decks, 'Visitors ashore, please!' and voices rose to a strident chorus. For a while the gangplanks were thronged; then they were empty, and the jostling crowd behind the barrier waved and called unintelligible things, and kept up a grin of good will. As the stevedores began to work at the ropes a flat-faced, somewhat befuddled young man arrived in a great hurry and was assisted up the gangplank by a porter and a taxi driver. The ship having swallowed him as impassively as though he were a missionary for Beirut, a low, portentous vibration began. The pier with its faces commenced to slide by, and for a moment the boat was just a piece accidentally split off from it; then the faces became remote, voiceless, and the pier was one among many yellow blurs along the water front. Now the harbour flowed swiftly toward the sea.

On a northern parallel of latitude a hurricane was forming

and moving south by southeast preceded by a strong west wind. On its course it was destined to swamp the *Peter I. Eudin* of Amsterdam, with a crew of sixty-six, to break a boom on the largest boat in the world, and to bring grief and want to the wives of several hundred seamen. This liner, leaving New York Sunday evening, would enter the zone of the storm Tuesday, and of the hurricane late Wednesday night.

2

Tuesday afternoon Adrian and Eva paid their first visit to the smoking-room. This was not in accord with their intentions – they had 'never wanted to see a cocktail again' after leaving America – but they had forgotten the staccato loneliness of ships, and all activity centred about the bar. So they went in for just a minute.

It was full. There were those who had been there since luncheon, and those who would be there until dinner, not to mention a faithful few who had been there since nine this morning. It was a prosperous assembly, taking its recreation at bridge, solitaire, detective stories, alcohol, argument and love. Up to this point you could have matched it in the club or casino life of any country, but over it all played a repressed nervous energy, a barely disguised impatience that extended to old and young alike. The cruise had begun, and they had enjoyed the beginning, but the show was not varied enough to last six days, and already they wanted it to be over.

At a table near them Adrian saw the pretty girl who had stared at him on the deck the first night. Again he was fascinated by her loveliness; there was no mist upon the brilliant gloss that gleamed through the smoky confusion of the room. He and Eva had decided from the passenger list that she was probably 'Miss Elizabeth D'Amido and maid', and he had heard her called Betsy as he walked past a deck-tennis game. Among the young people with her was the flat-nosed youth who had been 'poured on board', the night of their departure; yesterday he had walked the deck morosely, but he was apparently reviving. Miss D'Amido whispered something to him, and he looked over at the Smiths with curious eyes. Adrian was new enough at being a celebrity to turn self-consciously away.

'There's a little roll. Do you feel it ?' Eva demanded.

'Perhaps we'd better split a pint of champagne.'

While he gave the order a short colloquy was taking place at the other table; presently a young man rose and came over to them.

'Isn't this Mr Adrian Smith ?'

'Yes.'

'We wondered if we couldn't put you down for the deck-tennis tournament. We're going to have a deck-tennis tournament.'

'Why –' Adrian hesitated.

'My name's Stacomb,' burst out the young man. 'We all know your – your plays or whatever it is, and all that – and we wondered if you wouldn't like to come over to our table.'

Somewhat overwhelmed, Adrian laughed : Mr Stacomb, glib, soft, slouching, waited; evidently under the impression that he had delivered himself of a graceful compliment.

Adrian, understanding that, too, replied : 'Thanks, but perhaps you'd better come over here.'

'We've got a bigger table.'

'But we're older and more – more settled.'

The young man laughed kindly, as if to say, 'That's all right.'

'Put me down,' said Adrian. 'How much do I owe you ?'

'One buck. Call me Stac.'

'Why ?' asked Adrian, startled.

'It's shorter.'

When he had gone they smiled broadly.

'Heavens,' Eva gasped, 'I believe they are coming over.'

They were. With a great draining of glasses, calling of waiters, shuffling of chairs, three boys and two girls moved to the Smiths' table. If there was any diffidence, it was confined to the hosts; for the new additions gathered around them eagerly, eyeing Adrian with respect – too much respect – as if to say : 'This was probably a mistake and won't be amusing, but maybe we'll get something out of it to help us in our after life, like at school.'

In a moment Miss D'Amido changed seats with one of the men and placed her radiant self at Adrian's side, looking at him with manifest admiration.

'I fell in love with you the minute I saw you,' she said audibly and without self-consciousness; 'so I'll take all the blame for butting in. I've seen your play four times.'

Adrian called a waiter to take their orders.

'You see,' continued Miss D'Amido, 'we're going into a storm, and you might be prostrated the rest of the trip, so I couldn't take any chances.'

He saw that there was no undertone or innuendo in what she said, nor the need of any. The words themselves were enough, and the deference with which she neglected the young men and bent her politeness on him was somehow very touching. A little glow went over him; he was having rather more than a pleasant time.

Eva was less entertained; but the flat-nosed young man, whose name was Butterworth, knew people that she did, and that seemed to make the affair less careless and casual. She did not like meeting new people unless they had 'something to contribute', and she was often bored by the great streams of them, of all types and conditions and classes, that passed through Adrian's life. She herself 'had everything' – which is to say that she was well endowed with talents and with charm – and the mere novelty of people did not seem a sufficient reason for eternally offering everything up to them.

Half an hour later when she rose to go and see the children, she was content that the episode was over. It was colder on deck, with a damp that was almost rain, and there was a perceptible motion. Opening the door of her state-room she was surprised to find the cabin steward sitting languidly on her bed, his head slumped upon the upright pillow. He looked at her listlessly as she came in, but made no move to get up.

'When you've finished your nap you can fetch me a new pillow-case,' she said briskly.

Still the man didn't move. She perceived then that his face was green.

'You can't be seasick in here,' she announced firmly. 'You go and lie down in your own quarters.'

'It's me side,' he said faintly. He tried to rise, gave out a little rasping sound of pain and sank back again. Eva rang for the stewardess.

A steady pitch, toss, roll had begun in earnest and she felt no sympathy for the steward, but only wanted to get him out as quick as possible. It was outrageous for a member of the crew to be seasick. When the stewardess came in Eva tried to explain this, but now her own head was whirring, and throwing herself on the bed, she covered her eyes.

'It's his fault,' she groaned when the man was assisted from the room. 'I was all right and it made me sick to look at him. I wish he'd die.'

In a few minutes Adrian came in.

'Oh, but I'm sick!' she cried.

'Why, you poor baby.' He leaned over and took her in his arms. 'Why didn't you tell me?'

'I was all right upstairs, but there was a steward – Oh, I'm too sick to talk.'

'You'd better have dinner in bed.'

'Dinner! Oh, my heavens!'

He waited solicitously, but she wanted to hear his voice, to have it drown out the complaining sound of the beams.

'Where've you been?'

'Helping to sign up people for the tournament.'

'Will they have it if it's like this? Because if they do I'll just lose for you.'

He didn't answer; opening her eyes, she saw that he was frowning.

'I didn't know you were going in the doubles,' he said.

'Why, that's the only fun.'

'I told the D'Amido girl I'd play with her.'

'Oh.'

'I didn't think. You know I'd much rather play with you.'

'Why didn't you, then?' she asked coolly.

'It never occurred to me.'

She remembered that on their honeymoon they had been in the finals and won a prize. Years passed. But Adrian never frowned in this regretful way unless he felt a little guilty. He stumbled about, getting his dinner clothes out of the trunk, and she shut her eyes.

When a particular violent lurch startled her awake again he was dressed and tying his tie. He looked healthy and fresh, and his eyes were bright.

'Well, how about it?' he inquired. 'Can you make it, or no?'

'No.'

'Can I do anything for you before I go?'

'Where are you going?'

'Meeting those kids in the bar. Can I do anything for you?'

'No.'

'Darling, I hate to leave you like this.'

'Don't be silly. I just want to sleep.'

That solicitous frown – when she knew he was crazy to be out and away from the close cabin. She was glad when the door closed. The thing to do was to sleep, sleep.

Up – down – sideways. Hey there, not so far! Pull her round the corner there! Now roll her, right – left – Crea-eak! Wrench! Swoop!

Some hours later Eva was dimly conscious of Adrian bending over her. She wanted him to put his arms around her and draw her up out of this dizzy lethargy, but by the time she was fully awake the cabin was empty. He had looked in and gone. When she awoke next the cabin was dark and he was in bed.

The morning was fresh and cool, and the sea was just enough calmer to make Eva think she could get up. They breakfasted in the cabin and with Adrian's help she accomplished an unsatisfactory makeshift toilet and they went up on the boat deck. The tennis tournament had already begun and was furnishing action for a dozen amateur movie cameras, but the majority of passengers were represented by lifeless bundles in deck chairs beside untasted trays.

Adrian and Miss D'Amido played their first match. She was deft and graceful; blatantly well. There was even more warmth behind her ivory skin than there had been the day before. The strolling first officer stopped and talked to her; half a dozen men whom she couldn't have known three days ago called her Betsy. She was already the pretty girl of the voyage, the cynosure of starved ship's eyes.

But after a while Eva preferred to watch the gulls in the wireless masts and the slow slide of the roll-top sky. Most of the passengers looked silly with their movie cameras that they had all rushed to get and now didn't know what to use for, but the sailors painting the lifeboat stanchions were quiet and beaten and sympathetic, and probably wished, as she did, that the voyage was over.

Butterworth sat down on the deck beside her chair.

'They're operating on one of the stewards this morning. Must be terrible in this sea.'

'Operating? What for?' she asked listlessly.

'Appendicitis. They have to operate now because we're going into worse weather. That's why they're having the ship's party tonight.'

'Oh, the poor man!' she cried, realizing it must be her steward.

Adrian was showing off now by being very courteous and thoughtful in the game.

'Sorry. Did you hurt yourself?... No, it was my fault.... You better put on your coat right away, pardner, or you'll catch cold.'

The match was over and they had won. Flushed and hearty, he came up to Eva's chair.

'How do you feel?'

'Terrible.'

'Winners are buying a drink in the bar,' he said apologetically.

'I'm coming, too,' Eva said, but an immediate dizziness made her sink back in her chair.

'You'd better stay here. I'll send you up something.'

She felt that his public manner had hardened towards her slightly.

'You'll come back?'

'Oh, right away.'

She was alone on the boat deck, save for a solitary ship's officer who slanted obliquely as he paced the bridge. When the cocktail arrived she forced herself to drink it, and felt better. Trying to distract her mind with pleasant things, she reached back to the sanguine talks that she and Adrian had had before sailing: There was the little villa in Brittany, the children learning French – that was all she could think of now – the little villa in Brittany, the children learning French – so she repeated the words over and over to herself until they became as meaningless as the wide white sky. The why of their being here had suddenly eluded her; she felt unmotivated, accidental, and she wanted Adrian to come back quick, all responsive and tender, to reassure her. It was in the hope that there was some secret of graceful living, some real compensation for the lost, careless confidence of twenty-one, that they were going to spend a year in France.

The day passed darkly, with fewer people around and a wet sky falling. Suddenly it was five o'clock, and they were all in the bar again, and Mr Butterworth was telling her about his past. She took a good deal of champagne, but she was seasick dimly through it, as if the illness was her soul trying to struggle up through some thickening incrustation of abnormal life.

'You're my idea of a Greek goddess, physically,' Butterworth was saying.

It was pleasant to be Mr Butterworth's idea of a Greek goddess physically, but where was Adrian? He and Miss D'Amido had gone out on a forward deck to feel the spray. Eva heard herself promising to get out her colours and paint the Eiffel Tower on Butterworth's shirt front for the party tonight.

When Adrian and Betsy D'Amido, soaked with spray, opened the door with difficulty against the driving wind and came into the now-covered security of the promenade deck, they stopped and turned toward each other.

'Well?' she said. But he only stood with his back to the rail, looking at her, afraid to speak. She was silent, too, because she wanted him to be first; so for a moment nothing happened. Then she made a step towards him, and he took her in his arms and kissed her forehead.

'You're just sorry for me, that's all.' She began to cry a little. 'You're just being kind.'

'I feel terribly about it.' His voice was taut and trembling.

'Then kiss me.'

The deck was empty. He bent over her swiftly.

'No, really kiss me.'

He could not remember when anything had felt so young and fresh as her lips. The rain lay, like tears shed for him, upon the softly shining porcelain cheeks. She was all new and immaculate, and her eyes were wild.

'I love you,' she whispered. 'I can't help loving you, can I? When I first saw you – oh, not on the boat, but over a year ago – Grace Heally took me to a rehearsal and suddenly you jumped up in the second row and began telling them what to do. I wrote you a letter and tore it up.'

'We've got to go.'

She was weeping as they walked along the deck. Once more, imprudently, she held up her face to him at the door of her cabin. His blood was beating through him in wild tumult as he walked on to the bar.

He was thankful that Eva scarcely seemed to notice him or to know that he had been gone. After a moment he pretended an interest in what she was doing.

'What's that?'

'She's painting the Eiffel Tower on my shirt front for to-night,' explained Butterworth.

'There,' Eva laid away her brush and wiped her hands. 'How's that?'

'A *chef-d'oeuvre*.'

Her eyes swept around the watching group, lingered casually upon Adrian.

'You're wet. Go and change.'

'You come too.'

'I want another champagne cocktail.'

'You've had enough. It's time to dress for the party.'

Unwilling she closed her paints and preceded him.

'Stacomb's got a table for nine,' he remarked as they walked along the corridor.

'The younger set,' she said with unnecessary bitterness. 'Oh, the younger set. And you just having the time of your life – with a child.'

They had a long discussion in the cabin, unpleasant on her part and evasive on his, which ended when the ship gave a sudden gigantic heave, and Eva, the edge worn off her champagne, felt ill again. There was nothing to do but to have a cocktail in the cabin, and after that they decided to go to the party – she believed him now, or she didn't care.

Adrian was ready first – he never wore fancy dress.

'I'll go on up. Don't be long.'

'Wait for me, please; it's rocking so.'

He sat down on a bed, concealing his impatience.

'You don't mind waiting, do you? I don't want to parade up there all alone.'

She was taking a tuck in an oriental costume rented from the barber.

'Ships make people feel crazy,' she said. 'I think they're awful.'

'Yes,' he muttered absently.

'When it gets very bad I pretend I'm in the top of a tree, rocking to and fro. But finally I get pretending everything, and finally I have to pretend I'm sane when I know I'm not.'

'If you get thinking that way you will go crazy.'

'Look, Adrian.' She held up the string of pearls before clasping them on. 'Aren't they lovely?'

In Adrian's impatience she seemed to move around the cabin like a figure in a slow-motion picture. After a moment he demanded :

'Are you going to be long? It's stifling in here.'

'You go on!' she fired up.

'I don't want –'

'Go on, please! You just make me nervous trying to hurry me.'

With a show of reluctance he left her. After a moment's hesitation he went down a flight to a deck below and knocked at a door.

'Betsy.'

'Just a minute.'

She came out in the corridor attired in a red pea-jacket and trousers borrowed from the elevator boy.

'Do elevator boys have fleas?' she demanded. 'I've got everything in the world on under this as a precaution.'

'I had to see you,' he said quickly.

'Careful,' she whispered. 'Mrs Worden, who's supposed to be chaperoning me, is across the way. She's sick.'

'I'm sick for you.'

They kissed suddenly, clung close together in the narrow corridor, swaying to and fro with the motion of the ship.

'Don't go away,' she murmured.

'I've got to. I've –'

Her youth seemed to flow into him, bearing him up into a delicate romantic ecstasy that transcended passion. He couldn't relinquish it; he had discovered something that he had thought was lost with his own youth forever. As he walked along the passage he knew that he had stopped thinking, no longer dared to think.

He met Eva going into the bar.

'Where've you been?' she asked with a strained smile.

'To see about the table.'

She was lovely; her cool distinction conquered the trite costume and filled him with a resurgence of approval and pride. They sat down at a table.

The gale was rising hour by hour and the mere traversing of a passage had become a rough matter. In every stateroom trunks were lashed to the washstands, and the *Vestris* disaster was being reviewed in detail by nervous ladies, tossing, ill and wretched, upon their beds. In the smoking-room a stout gentleman had been hurled backward and suffered a badly cut head; and now the lighter chairs and tables were stacked and roped against the wall.

The crowd who had donned fancy dress and were dining together had swollen to about sixteen. The only remaining qualification for membership was the ability to reach the smoking-room. They ranged from a Groton-Harvard lawyer to an ungrammatical broker they had nicknamed Gyp the Blood, but distinctions had disappeared; for the moment they were samurai, chosen from several hundred for their triumphant resistance to the storm.

The gala dinner, overhung sardonically with lanterns and streamers, was interrupted by great communal slides across the room, precipitate retirements and spilled wine, while the ship roared and complained that under the panoply of a palace it was a ship after all. Upstairs afterward a dozen couples tried to dance, shuffling and galloping here and there in a crazy fandango, thrust around fantastically by a will alien to their own. In view of the condition of tortured hundreds below, there grew to be something indecent about it like a revel in a house of mourning, and presently there was an egress of the ever-dwindling survivors towards the bar.

As the evening passed, Eva's feeling of unreality increased. Adrian had disappeared – presumably with Miss D'Amido – and her mind, distorted by illness and champagne, began to enlarge upon the fact; annoyance changed slowly to dark and brooding anger, grief to desperation. She had never tried to bind Adrian, never needed to – for they were serious people, with all sorts of mutual interests, and satisfied with each other – but this was a breach of the contract, this was cruel. How could he think that she didn't know?

It seemed several hours later that he leaned over her chair in the bar where she was giving some woman an impassioned lecture upon babies, and said:

'Eva, we'd better turn in.'

Her lip curled. 'So that you can leave me there and then come back to your eighteen-year –'

'Be quiet.'

'I won't come to bed.'

'Very well. Good night.'

More time passed and the people at the table changed. The stewards wanted to close up the room, and thinking of Adrian – her Adrian – off somewhere saying tender things to someone fresh and lovely, Eva began to cry.

'But he's gone to bed,' her last attendants assured her. 'We saw him go.'

She shook her head. She knew better. Adrian was lost. The long seven-year dream was broken. Probably she was punished for something she had done; as this thought occurred to her the shrieking timbers overhead began to mutter that she had guessed at last. This was for the selfishness to her mother, who hadn't wanted her to marry Adrian; for all the sins and omissions of her life. She stood up, saying she must go out and get some air.

The deck was dark and drenched with wind and rain. The ship pounded through valleys, fleeing from black mountains of water that roared towards it. Looking out at the night, Eva saw that there was no chance for them unless she could make atonement, propitiate the storm. It was Adrian's love that was demanded of her. Deliberately she unclasped her pearl necklace, lifted it to her lips – for she knew that with it went the freshest, fairest part of her life – and flung it out into the gale.

3

When Adrian awoke it was lunchtime, but he knew that some heavier sound than the bugle had called him up from his deep sleep. Then he realized that the trunk had broken loose from its lashings and was being thrown back and forth between a wardrobe and Eva's bed. With an exclamation he jumped up, but she was unharmed – still in costume and stretched out in deep sleep. When the steward had helped him secure the trunk, Eva opened a single eye.

'How are you?' he demanded, sitting on the side of her bed.

She closed the eye, opened it again.

'We're in a hurricane now,' he told her. 'The steward says it's the worst he's seen in twenty years.'

'My head,' she muttered. 'Hold my head.'

'How?'

'In front. My eyes are going out. I think I'm dying.'

'Nonsense. Do you want the doctor?'

She gave a funny little gasp that frightened him; he rang and sent the steward for the doctor.

The young doctor was pale and tired. There was a stubble of beard upon his face. He bowed curtly as he came in and, turning to Adrian, said with scant ceremony:

'What's the matter?'

'My wife doesn't feel well.'

'Well, what is it you want – a bromide?'

A little annoyed by his shortness, Adrian said: 'You'd better examine her and see what she needs.'

'She needs a bromide,' said the doctor. 'I've given orders that she is not to have any more to drink on this ship.'

'Why not?' demanded Adrian in astonishment.

'Don't you know what happened last night?'

'Why, no, I was asleep.'

'Mrs Smith wandered around the boat for an hour, not knowing what she was doing. A sailor was sent to follow her, and then the medical stewardess tried to get her to bed, and your wife insulted her.'

'Oh, my heavens!' cried Eva faintly.

'The nurse and I had both been up all night with Steward Carton, who died this morning.' He picked up his case. 'I'll send down a bromide for Mrs Smith. Good-bye.'

For a few minutes there was silence in the cabin. Then Adrian put his arm around her quickly.

'Never mind,' he said. 'We'll straighten it out.'

'I remember now.' Her voice was an awed whisper. 'My pearls. I threw them overboard.'

'Threw them overboard!'

'Then I began looking for you.'

'But I was here in bed.'

'I didn't believe it; I thought you were with that girl.'

'She collapsed during dinner. I was taking a nap down here.'

Frowning, he rang the bell and asked the steward for luncheon and a bottle of beer.

'Sorry, but we can't serve any beer to your cabin, sir.'

When he went out Adrian exploded: 'This is an outrage. You were simply crazy from that storm and they can't be so highhanded. I'll see the captain.'

'Isn't that awful?' Eva murmured. 'The poor man died.'

She turned over and began to sob into her pillow. There was a knock at the door.

'Can I come in?'

The assiduous Mr Butterworth, surprisingly healthy and immaculate, came into the crazily tipping cabin.

'Well, how's the mystic?' he demanded of Eva. 'Do you remember praying to the elements in the bar last night?'

'I don't want to remember anything about last night.'

They told him about the stewardess, and with the telling the situation lightened; they all laughed together.

'I'm going to get you some beer to have with your luncheon,' Butterworth said. 'You ought to get up on deck.'

'Don't go,' Eva said. 'You look so cheerful and nice.'

'Just for ten minutes.'

When he had gone, Adrian rang for two baths.

'The thing is to put on our best clothes and walk proudly three times around the deck,' he said.

'Yes.' After a moment she added abstractedly: 'I like that young man. He was awfully nice to me last night when you'd disappeared.'

The bath steward appeared with the information that bathing was too dangerous today. They were in the midst of the wildest hurricane on the North Atlantic in ten years; there were two broken arms this morning from attempts to take baths. An elderly lady had been thrown down a staircase and was not expected to live. Furthermore, they had received the SOS signal from several boats this morning.

'Will we go to help them?'

'They're all behind us, sir, so we have to leave them to the *Mauretania*. If we tried to turn in this sea the portholes would be smashed.'

This array of calamities minimized their own troubles. Having eaten a sort of luncheon and drunk the beer provided by Butterworth, they dressed and went on deck.

Despite the fact that it was only possible to progress step by step, holding on to rope or rail, more people were abroad than on the day before. Fear had driven them from their cabins, where the trunks bumped and the waves pounded the portholes, and they awaited momentarily the call to the boats. Indeed, as Adrian and Eva stood on the transverse deck above the second class, there was a bugle call, followed by a gathering of stewards and stewardesses on the deck below. But the boat was sound; it had outlasted one of its cargo – Steward James Carton was being buried at sea.

It was very British and sad. There were the rows of stiff, disciplined men and women standing in the driving rain, and there was a shape covered by the flag of the Empire that lived by the sea. The chief purser read the service, a hymn was sung, the body slid off into the hurricane. With Eva's burst of wild weeping for this humble end, some last string snapped within her. Now she really didn't care. She responded eagerly when Butterworth suggested that he get some champagne to their cabin. Her mood worried Adrian; she wasn't used to so much drinking and he wondered what he ought to do. At his suggestion that they sleep instead, she merely laughed, and the bromide the doctor had sent stood untouched on the washstand. Pretending to listen to the insipidities of several Mr Stacombs, he watched her; to his surprise and discomfort she seemed on intimate and even sentimental terms with Butterworth and he wondered if this was a form of revenge for his attention to Betsy D'Amido.

The cabin was full of smoke, the voices went on incessantly, the suspension of activity, the waiting for the storm's end, was getting on his nerves. They had been at sea only four days; it was like a year.

The two Mr Stacombs left finally, but Butterworth remained. Eva was urging him to go for another bottle of champagne.

'We've had enough,' objected Adrian. 'We ought to go to bed.'

'I won't go to bed!' she burst out. 'You must be crazy! You play around all you want, and then, when I find somebody I – I like, you want to put me to bed.'

'You're hysterical.'

'On the contrary, I've never been so sane.'

'I think you'd better leave us, Butterworth,' Adrian said. 'Eva doesn't know what she's saying.'

'He won't go. I won't let him go.' She clasped Butterworth's hand passionately. 'He's the only person that's been half decent to me.'

'You'd better go, Butterworth,' repeated Adrian.

The young man looked at him uncertainly.

'It seems to me you're being unjust to your wife,' he ventured.

'My wife isn't herself.'

'That's no reason for bullying her.'

Adrian lost his temper. 'You get out of here!' he cried.

The two men looked at each other for a moment in silence. Then Butterworth turned to Eva, said, 'I'll be back later,' and left the cabin.

'Eva, you've got to pull yourself together,' said Adrian when the door closed.

She didn't answer, looked at him from sullen, half-closed eyes.

'I'll order dinner here for us both and then we'll try to get some sleep.'

'I want to go up and send a wireless.'

'Who to?'

'Some Paris lawyer. I want a divorce.'

In spite of his annoyance, he laughed. 'Don't be silly.'

'Then I want to see the children.'

'Well, go and see them. I'll order dinner.'

He waited for her in the cabin twenty minutes. Then

impatiently he opened the door across the corridor; the nurse told him that Mrs Smith had not been there.

With a sudden prescience of disaster he ran upstairs, glanced in the bar, the salons, even knocked at Butterworth's door. Then a quick round of the decks, feeling his way through the black spray and rain. A sailor stopped him at a network of ropes.

'Orders are no one goes by, sir. A wave has gone over the wireless room.'

'Have you seen a lady?'

'There was a young lady here –' He stopped and glanced around. 'Hello, she's gone.'

'She went up the stairs!' Adrian said anxiously. 'Up to the wireless room!'

The sailor ran up to the boat deck; stumbling and slipping, Adrian followed. As he cleared the protected sides of the companionway, a tremendous body struck the boat a staggering blow and, as she keeled over to an angle of forty-five degrees, he was thrown in a helpless roll down the drenched deck, to bring up dizzy and bruised against a stanchion.

'Eva!' he called. His voice was soundless in the black storm. Against the faint light of the wirless-room window he saw the sailor making his way forward.

'Eva!'

The wind blew him like a sail up against a lifeboat. Then there was another shuddering crash, and high over his head, over the very boat, he saw a gigantic, glittering white wave, and in the split second that it balanced there he became conscious of Eva, standing beside a ventilator twenty feet away. Pushing out from the stanchion, he lunged desperately toward her, just as the wave broke with a smashing roar. For a moment the rushing water was five feet deep, sweeping with enormous force towards the side, and then a human body was washed against him, and frantically he clutched it and was swept with it back towards the rail. He felt his body bump against it, but desperately he held on to his burden; then, as the ship rocked slowly back, the two of them, still joined by his fierce grip, were rolled out exhausted on the wet planks. For a moment he knew no more.

4

Two days later, as the boat train moved tranquilly south toward Paris, Adrian tried to persuade his children to look out the window at the Norman countryside.

'It's beautiful,' he assured them. 'All the little farms like toys. Why, in heaven's name, won't you look?'

'I like the boat better,' said Estelle.

Her parents exchanged an infanticidal glance.

'The boat is still rocking for me,' Eva said with a shiver. 'Is it for you?'

'No. Somehow, it all seems a long way off. Even the passengers looked unfamiliar going through the customs.'

'Most of them hadn't appeared above ground before.'

He hesitated. 'By the way, I cashed Butterworth's cheque for him.'

'You're a fool. You'll never see the money again.'

'He must have needed it pretty badly or he would not have come to me.'

A pale and wan girl, passing along the corridor, recognized them and put her head through the doorway.

'How do you feel?'

'Awful.'

'Me, too,' agreed Miss D'Amido. 'I'm vainly hoping my fiancé will recognize me at the Gare du Nord. Do you know two waves went over the wireless room?'

'So we heard,' Adrian answered dryly.

She passed gracefully along the corridor and out of their life.

'The real truth is that none of it happened,' said Adrian after a moment. 'It was a nightmare – an incredibly awful nightmare.'

'Then, where are my pearls?'

'Darling, there are better pearls in Paris. I'll take the responsibility for those pearls. My real belief is that you saved the boat.'

'Adrian, let's never get to know anyone else, but just stay together always – just we two.'

He tucked her arm under his and they sat close. 'Who do you suppose those Adrian Smiths on the boat were?' he demanded. 'It certainly wasn't me.'

'Nor me.'

'It was two other people,' he said, nodding to himself. 'There are so many Smiths in this world.'